BEST BONDAGE EROTICA 2015

BEST
BONDAGE EROTICA
2015

Edited by

Rachel Kramer Bussel

Foreword by

Annabel Joseph

CLEiS
PRESS

Published in the United States by Cleis Press,
an imprint of Start Midnight, LLC,
609 Greenwich Street, Sixth Floor, New York, New York 10014.

Printed in the United States.
Cover design: Scott Idleman/Blink
Cover photograph: iStockphoto
Text design: Frank Wiedemann

First Edition.
10 9 8 7 6 5 4 3 2 1

Trade paper ISBN: 978-1-62778-089-6
E-book ISBN: 978-1-62778-104-6

CONTENTS

FOREWORD: THE MOMENT

Annabel Joseph

I've always had a thing for short stories.

I cut my teeth on Ernest Hemingway, then started on the O. Henry Award anthologies, containing the most notable short stories of each year. When I got older and kinkier, I started reading erotic anthologies, and oh, that was a wondrous discovery. The thrill of short stories and eroticism together...well. More on that in a sex. I mean, sec. Ahem.

My love for short stories isn't a time-saving thing—I'll read a bajillion-page book if it holds my interest. People who love short stories don't love them because they're short. They love them because they're sharp. Short story authors hone desire and emotion to a glittering, fine point and then jab you with it. *See? Do you see?*

As much as I love short stories, I generally write full-length novels, where there's lots of space to tell a complex story. Novels allow for twists and turns, for chapters' worth of buildup, but a short story demands brevity and finesse, and that fine, glittering point I mentioned earlier. Maybe it's better to call it a moment.

Oh, the *moment*.

In a short story, there is always that moment when you

realize something out of the ordinary is happening. It might be a sneaky, provocative tease of a reveal, or an earth-shattering shock that blows your mind. Either way, you're hooked, and you read on until you reach that fine, glittering point the author meant to poke you with. In erotic tales, the moment is almost always about fulfillment, or connection, or a realization of something about oneself. In the best moments, you, the reader, find pleasure or joy.

In bondage too, there is that moment when you find yourself trapped in rope or cuffs, or yarn, or plaster, or one of the other delightfully creative bondage methods in this volume. In the best cases, you'll feel yourself without recourse for getting away, and you'll think *Ah*, and *Oh*, and *What will happen to me now*, and *Will I be able to endure it? Will it change me?*

How?

Or perhaps you're the one doing the binding, and your moment arrives at the sound of your subject's pleasure. Or terror. Perhaps it's that moment when your gaze locks on your partner, and both of you realize, *Wow. We've created this moment together. We've created this magic between us, at least until the bonds let loose.*

The lovingly crafted erotic tales you're about to read also build to a moment. In some cases it's a quiet moment, and in others, a surprising or humorous moment. No matter what kind of moment, it will make you feel something. That's good bondage—and good short-story writing. If you're like me, you'll pause on the page to enjoy the desire, or discovery, or emotion. Perhaps you'll go back to reread and savor it again. Perhaps you'll even go off to find a partner to savor it with in a more hands-on way.

To me, short stories and bondage go together as perfectly as subject and rigger, as top and bottom, as Mistress or Master and slave, because they all strive to create these memorable moments. If you're reading this collection, you probably already agree with me. If you don't agree with me yet, read a few stories and you'll see.

I wish you many fine, glittering moments in reading, in bondage and in life. And if you haven't had any moments lately, perhaps it's time to start looking for them. I promise you'll find many inspiring ones in the pages of this book.

Annabel Joseph
New York Times bestselling author of *Comfort Object*

INTRODUCTION: BONDAGE AT HOME AND AWAY

Every year, different themes emerge from the submissions I receive for the *Best Bondage Erotica* series. This year bondage writers stuck close to home—literally. This year, I received stories like "Housewarming the Craftsman," by Daddy X, and "Stuck on You," by Jenne Davis, focused on housing, real estate and home improvement, that are both humorous and offer some creative forms of containment that prove you don't need a Red Room of Pain to make someone writhe. While in "Tying the Knot," by Rob Rosen, bondage gets mobile, there's a sweetness to this engagement story that tethers the protagonists close to each other, and their marital home. In "Bound to Lie" by Nichelle Gregory, two business adversaries battle it out in the boardroom for the ultimate form of control.

In these kinky tales, bondage happens as part of yoga, knitting, a birthday present, with a collar, a cage, duct tape, a webcam, and a very sexy pair of thighs. Bondage, in some cases, is in the eye and mind of the one being bound. It's what happens after these eager, curious, brave characters are trussed up, immobile, secure in their trappings, that makes for the most powerful sexual encounters of all.

Whatever form the bondage takes, each of the characters you'll read about in *Best Bondage Erotica 2015* struggles and delights in the power and intimacy invoked in the name of knowing one's place, literally and figuratively.

Rachel Kramer Bussel
Red Bank, New Jersey

THE CENTERPIECE

Erin Spillane

I stop at the open door of Greg's office and hesitate. Many nights with him are a surprise, and I have yet to experience one that I didn't like.

I am completely naked except for the ballerina heels on my feet, which are beautiful, with flowers made out of beads and lace covering the entire surface. I'm walking on the tips of my toes, making balancing extremely difficult, so my full concentration is on each step I take.

Inside, I can see Greg working at his desk. He is an utterly beautiful man, and he's all mine. Short black hair, deep-green eyes and a goatee that shapes his wide, full lips. His nose is straight and long and his cheekbones are prominent and high. He rarely shows any facial expression when we play, making it hard to determine his mood in the moment. He simply takes my breath away.

"Oh love, you are going to make such a beautiful centerpiece tonight," he says as he comes over to me and takes hold of my elbow, guiding me into the room.

I've been in this room many times over the past year, but tonight, there is an odd table over by the fireplace that I take a moment to study. It's a half circle, the flat end facing the fireplace, almost like a blackjack table. And where the dealer would stand is a pole straight out of a strip club. About a foot up from the table, attached to the pole, is a small shelf that sticks out toward the seats. Chains and leather straps dangle from all ends of the equipment. On the shelf, a rather large piece of metal sticks up, already wet with something, because it shines from the overhead light.

I stand there getting wet, thinking of what Greg plans on doing tonight. Arousal courses through me and I tingle all over, while my legs start to shake from the strain of standing in these heels and the excitement of what's going to happen.

Greg doesn't give me long to look over the table before he's urging me over to it.

"I bought this for you, love. I think you're going to like it. Now, up you go, stand on the table." His voice is calm, but his eyes shine with excitement.

I'll never tell him, but his eyes always give him away.

With his assistance, I stand on the table and look down at him for my next instructions.

He gestures for me to sit on the shelf with my back against the pole. I can see now that the metal piece on the shelf is actually a steel ribbed dildo. I carefully start to lower myself, letting the metal touch the entrance of my pussy, when he stops me with a hand on my ass.

"Now, love, that won't do. I have something else to fill that hole."

I stare at him in shock. There's no way that's going to fit in my anus. I look toward the door as if to escape, and Greg just chuckles. I wouldn't make it far if I ran, especially with these ballerina heels on. But to be honest, I wouldn't run from this night anyway. Greg would never hurt me.

I maneuver my body until the tip of the metal rests against my asscheeks. The heels make it impossible to push my body down any farther without falling. I look at Greg for help.

I know not to speak without permission when we play, but I don't have to worry. I trust Greg and he always seems to know when I need something.

"Let me take your weight," Greg says. The feel of his cool hands on my hips has goose bumps breaking out on my heated skin.

With his support, I move my feet to the side, until my ankles are at an odd angle and touch the table.

Greg pushes me down and the pain of being so full, so quick, sends an odd sensation through my body. It takes my breath away. My eyes water while my body tries to adjust to the large object in me.

"Breathe, love. Take a nice, deep breath for me."

I try, but it's hard. I end up taking short quick breaths, which earns me a hard swat on one of my nipples. I'm so wet, I should probably be embarrassed about my reaction, but as the pain works through my body it makes me feel so alive. Energized and eager for more.

Before my body adjusts to the invasion, a warm, tingling sensation starts to spread through my insides from the plug. I look up at Greg in horror, and he calmly stares at me. I bounce up and down to try and alleviate the burn, but Greg grabs one of my legs in his hand and swivels the pole around. The motion sends the metal deeper in my ass, holding me immobile. I dangle from the pole by just the piece in my ass and Greg's grip on one of my legs. The shelf between my leg digs into my thighs.

"I have a special lubricant I thought we'd use this time.

Remember the ginger lube we saw the other day? I bought it. I love watching you squirm on the pole. The feeling lasts for a while. Even after I get you down from there, we might have to wash you out to stop it. It has some cinnamon in it, too."

The thought of the lube worries me. No matter how much time has passed, new things still have the ability to frighten me.

I can't stop gyrating on the pole. I try to escape the heat but I can't; he won't let me. How long does he plan to keep me up here? How long will it last? And how will he clean it out later? The questions pelt my brain one after another. Tears squeeze from my eyes. I cry out without thinking, and it earns me another swat on my nipples.

"Grab the pole above you, and don't let go," he demands in a tone I can't ignore. I instantly grab hold of the pole above my head, no hesitation in my movement.

Greg takes hold of my legs above my knee, and I am so happy when he places my thighs on the shelf. The pressure lessens, and I feel some relief. The shelf is only large enough to hold me to my thighs, so my knees are bent and my toes point straight to the ground. His rough hands caress my legs before separating them until I am in a split position. The shelf is two pieces, one for each leg, and Greg reaches down to find the leather and metal straps to wrap around me from my upper thigh to above my knee. It doesn't take him long to complete the process, binding my legs and leaving me no give to close them.

I look down at the wide-open display I'm bound to. My pussy is completely bare, spread open with nothing to shield it or the anal plug that I sit on. Instinctively, I tighten my muscles to see if the shelf will move at all, but it's locked. My predicament settles in, and I shiver in bliss. I love this part, the point of no return.

Helpless.

Greg steps away from me and looks at his handiwork. When his gaze makes it to my face, one side of his mouth twitches slightly.

He turns to grab a chair that he pulls over in between my spread thighs and climbs onto it. This close, I can smell his subtle cologne, a smell that always comforts me. He reaches up to pry my hands from the pole and raises them even higher. Pulling my body taut, he shackles my wrists to the fur-lined cuffs that dangle from the top.

"Some of my friends are coming over tonight to go over some business. You're going to be our centerpiece. Centerpieces look so nice, and I think you might be the prettiest any of them has ever seen. Sometimes they smell nice. I have a feeling this will be one of those times." He reaches between my legs and swirls his finger in my opening. "Become the perfect centerpiece, and we'll have a wonderful night."

I give him a nod; I will be perfect. He smooths my hair back and kisses my forehead. Out of his back pocket he pulls a piece of fabric, which he wraps around my head and settles over my eyes. The fabric is thick, with no give. I can't see anything.

Without sight, my other senses are now amplified. I hear the chair scrape over the wood floor as he places it back at the table. His footsteps are soft, barely noticeable. And then everything goes silent and I strain to hear anything that will give away his location.

I'm not sure how long I sit there before I hear him walk back to me. Time has no meaning, not when I'm lost to every sensation my body has to experience. His breath warms my chest seconds before his mouth engulfs my nipple and he sucks, hard. Greg gives my other nipple the same treatment before rubbing something onto them. The burn begins immediately. It's the same lubricant from the plug, and my nipples immediately pucker. My body clenches with the pleasure of the heat, but it only lasts for a moment before he puts a nipple clamp on and screws it tight. He quickly places a clamp on my other nipple before I even feel the pain from the first one. With both clamps on and tightened, pain shoots through my chest and brings tears to my eyes. But I am still getting wetter.

All my muscles are so tight, I can barely draw a breath. I know I have to breathe through it, but it's hard. I think I am about to pass out from lack of oxygen.

But Greg knows this and barks out, "Breathe. Now." And because he told me, and I don't want to disappoint him, I do.

"The clamps match your heels. They have such beautiful flowers on them," he breathes into my ear.

I try to imagine what I look like. The clamps are heavy, pulling my breasts toward the floor. My chest is pushed out and pulled tight from the bonds at my legs and arms. I try to draw even, slow breaths so my breasts won't jiggle, but it doesn't matter how hard or shallow I breathe. With the heat and burning in my anus, I can't stop moving anyway. I don't have much room, but I take advantage of the space I do have. I'm not sure I could stop even if Greg told me to at this point.

"Only two more accessories, love. I can already hear the gentlemen downstairs." Even though my body is on fire, that statement sends a shiver through my body. I hear the men, too. Greg is serious. How exciting!

Something cold touches the mouth of my pussy and slowly, Greg pushes the device in. It's a tight squeeze with the large anal plug taking up so much room, but it goes in smoothly.

"Now this, this has those beautiful beaded flowers and butterflies hanging off the end. It looks like your greedy little mouth is a spring garden in full bloom. Lucky for us, it's so wet there we don't have to worry about watering them anytime soon. This piece has different vibrations but I'll let the gentlemen play with that."

Once he secures the new device to the plug so that it will stay in place, one of Greg's fingers gently plays with my pussy. I'm on the verge of coming when he pulls his fingers away and places them on my lips. I pull his fingers into my mouth and lap at them. It's an exotic experience to taste oneself and even though I don't think I'll ever get used to it, it doesn't bother me like it once did.

The pain from my nipples and the fullness in my ass and pussy have me silently begging to come. God, I wish he'd let me orgasm. I'd do anything at this point to fly over the edge. But Greg likes to drag our play out, and in the back of my mind, I know it will be so much better the longer I wait.

Something rubber touches my lips; I automatically open my mouth so Greg can push a gag in. Oval in shape, it almost touches the back of my throat, forcing me to breathe through my nose. My lips stretch wide to accommodate the intrusion, and my tongue is held immobile. A whimper escapes, but he just pats me on the thigh.

"Don't worry, love, this too has those beaded flowers decorating it. It is absolutely lovely." Something heavy is placed on my head, like a crown. "And so you are complete head to toe, here's a small headpiece in the same design. Ah, stunning, you are absolutely stunning."

Greg steps away, then stops. I can feel the heat of his gaze as he looks at me. I know Greg finds me beautiful and that makes me almost preen in pride. I hope his friends do, too.

I lose my sense of balance for a moment when the pole is turned. I assume I'm now facing the table. In the distance I hear the office door close. Greg has gone to get his friends.

Left to my thoughts, my arousal subsides some when I

think about how close my body is to where the chairs are placed. The table is rather small; all they would have to do is reach over slightly to touch me. I am chained up, completely adorned, and any number of men are coming to sit at the table that I am the centerpiece of. He has bound almost every part of my body.

My anus and nipples burn but the feeling spreading through my body from those places is amazing. I feel like I am on fire in the best possible way. If the gag weren't in my mouth, they would hear my harsh pants when they arrive. I remind myself to breathe slow and steady.

I imagine I make a beautiful picture with my small frame, bound and aroused. Oh, how I wish I could see myself, but I will have to leave it up to the men to judge.

These men and Greg will see me as a centerpiece and for tonight, I am. Tomorrow, it's back to the real world and a computer. But I will wring every ounce of pleasure I can out of tonight.

My body is flushed and covered in a sheen of sweat. Knowing people will see me like this has cream gushing from my body around the vibrator inside me.

When I hear them walking in the hallway, my breath catches. It's showtime.

The door opens and the footfalls get closer. No one speaks, so I have no idea how many people are here. There are multiple footsteps though and it sounds like all five chairs are pulled from the table. I hold my breath, trying to hear more, but the room falls silent.

I start to squirm in my prison again, every inch of my body on fire. I have no idea what is happening or what I am to expect and in my mind, I try to picture the people in the room. Men and maybe some women, watching me. It is a heady concept. One I wish to hold on to. I feel beautiful and in control of the room. But that doesn't last long.

Soft murmurs fill the space around me, but I'm so focused on my own predicament, their words don't make sense. Every part of my body is held in tight to the pole. I am a centerpiece, not a participant of the conversation. And I love it.

I know time passes, but I don't know how long it is that I sit here, waiting. Waiting for what, I can't fathom. Maybe nothing. I am, after all, part of the decorations. And decorations don't usually receive much besides a passing glance and possibly appreciation.

Paper rustles, voices ebb and flow. The smells of cologne and perfume invade my senses. I sit in the middle of it all, trying hard not to move too much, yet unable to control myself.

Finally, calloused fingers start to stroke my pussy and I feel other fingers fiddle with the vibrator and turn it on. It starts to wiggle inside of me. Not vibrations, just a movement, and I gasp. A set of hands grabs hold of the clamps on my nipples and pulls straight out. I moan long and loud behind the gag in my mouth.

Someone from behind swats my ass, which means there could be more than the five men I had originally estimated to be in the room.

I suck on the gag so as not to make any more noise. Centerpieces don't make noise. Hands pet and stroke me from my arms down to my ankles. I try to concentrate and count how many, but the pleasure is sending my mind into a fog. There is one hand on each of my arms, and one hand on each of my calves. Other hands stroke my thighs, while someone's fingers play with my pussy. Rough hands caress my belly and breasts, too.

They are touching me everywhere and I give up trying to figure it out. I let myself sink into the sensation, enjoying each stroke, swat and pet.

The hand at my pussy starts to pinch and stretch my lips around the vibrator, over and over again. The ones playing with my breasts are gentle and soft, caressing the mounds and jarring the clamps on every pass. A pair of lips starts to kiss around the gag in my mouth. Oh, how I wish that the gag were gone. I wish I could kiss the rough lips so close to mine. The intimacy of the act always makes me wet and hungry for more.

Someone turns the vibrator on—a hard, fast massage. I start to pant again. I squirm in my bonds for all I'm worth, trying to reach the pinnacle. I must look like a spectacle, but I don't care. I can't care. My body has its own agenda and it's begging for relief. Between the heat, the caresses and the vibrator now on high, I can hardly even concentrate. I've lost my mind; I wouldn't be coherent if I could talk.

As my body flies higher and higher, tears leak from my eyes with my frustration. I am so close, just a few more moments. If only one of them would touch my clit.

And yet there is nothing I can do. I'm tied down tight and stuffed full. I can hardly move to give myself the additional stimulation needed to come.

I lose track of time as I strive to reach climax. My body becomes sore, and I can't work the kinks out.

Finally, finally, one of the people in the room pinches my clit between thick fingers. Someone else pulls a clamp off my nipple, and I start to come immediately. The blood rushing back to my nipple hurts so good, I'm sure I passed out for a moment. I've never felt anything so intense in my life. I've never been so high. I'm having trouble breathing. Shocks keep flowing through me, and I'm now bound to the pleasure my body is experiencing.

As the pleasure slowly wears away, I start to feel the pain in my limbs from being in this position for too long. My nerves scream at me to move, but I can't until they let me down.

The other nipple clamp comes off and two mouths latch on to soothe my nipples. They're so sore and the feeling of the lips sucking them isn't really that pleasurable, but I enjoy the roughness and pain.

The vibrator is pulled from pussy, but I still feel the vibrations move through my body. It has gone on for so long, I know I'll feel the vibrations long into the night. Hands unlock the straps along my legs, and someone lowers my poor arms.

Then I hear footsteps leaving the room. The door closes and Greg takes my blindfold off. I blink, trying to focus on his face. When I see his brilliant smile, I want to collapse.

"Beautiful," he whispers before taking me off the pole and cradling me to his chest.

Carrying my sore, pleasured body to the couch, he holds and rocks me until I fall asleep.

AN UNFORGETTABLE RIDE

Elise Hepner

The tiny electronic ping thrummed through her nerve endings, competing against the claustrophobia of purring engines, honking horns, and the deep chatter of pedestrians lining the sidewalks in gobs. Anna was hyper-focused, to the point where each sound almost hurt as she huddled in the squeaky, fake-leather cab seat. More than anything she wanted to pull the scratchy trench more securely around her nakedness—but the ropes stopped her. Hank had been thorough with his binding, as always. Her wrists chaffed from the delicious friction and she butted her nose against the simple silk blindfold, while knowing the action would get her a whole lot of nothing in the way of results. At least she could *pretend* she was more in control—even if she loved being out of it. Spinning, churning stomach, adrenaline making her voice thready and her hands shake: sweet ol' discipline.

Tonight Hank whistled in the driver's seat of the cab, making a jerky left turn that bounced her in the seat. Her ankles were cuffed with a spreader bar, leaving her no way to snatch any traction from the slick mats at her feet. Instead, all she could do was wait. Every second her thoughts grew more scattered, more certain Hank's game was all a weird joke.

"Time for our first customer, babe." Hank's voice trickled in through the partition and Anna's hands clenched together, body taut as a shudder ripped up her spine. "You ready?"

"Ready for what? What are we doing?" There wasn't a way to keep the tremulous note from her voice. "Hank? Hank!"

He jerked the wheel to the right and the cab slowed to a stop. Anna nearly choked, her throat went so tight at the idea—at the thought—

"Hank, are you really...you can't be serious! Babe! What... what the hell?"

"Do you trust me?"

"Yes!" she hissed out.

But not before the jerk of the door made her start. The smooth, cold kiss of air pressed through her light trench coat against her nakedness. She licked her lips, coming away with the unpleasant taste of the red lipstick Hank had applied after she'd been blindfolded. A Trollop Red, supposedly. Colors were the least of her worries as the seat moved with the weight of another person and Anna both threw back her shoulders while also pulling away the barest inch. The slap of spicy masculine cologne seeped through the cab. She heard a rough, grating chuckle that would have been sexy if she could see the whole package; instead, it set every inch of her body on alert.

"Nice." The stranger's voice had a bass growl with a Southern drawl and he made a purely masculine noise of approval in the back of his throat. "May I, Hank?"

At least Hank knew the man. Not a pure stranger. Like that was any real comfort while Anna pressed against the back of the cab's seat, nestled against the loose springs. Despite herself, she got a little wet when the cab jerked away from the curb.

No turning back; Hank wouldn't listen, wouldn't have an end to whatever plan he'd cooked up.

"What's mine is yours." Hank swore at someone on the road and swerved to the left.

With her boyfriend's permission the stranger's hand landed like a slap on her thigh, trailing goose bumps all along her upper body as she shivered in her bonds. Nothing made sense, but everything was blindingly clear. She struggled with a whimper, even while her nipples peaked so the coarse fabric rubbing against them made her teeth clench until her jaw ached. His finger drew small circles on her inner thigh. His touch was warm and weighted, with a press that was full of unspoken intentions while the cab jerked and jostled its way through busy streets.

"If someone got a look inside..." She tried to speak louder than a whisper, but the air was caught in her lungs, taken away by his all-consuming presence. The stranger sunk into her pores until he was the only thing she was aware of while his fingers drew complicated designs on her naked skin.

"Let 'em look."

Before she could get out another word his fingers skimmed up, palm clenching over her bare, slick pussy. She jumped, crying out, unable to close her legs to the intrusion, torn between excitement and shame that he would probably sense her arousal on his slow and exploratory fingers while he played her pussy as if it were a toy.

"Shit," she swore, eyes half-lidded behind her blindfold.

Unable to keep her head while her pulse throbbed against her temples and made her ears ring, she ground up into the pressure of his hand. She groaned, goaded by her base impulses. With a small grunt his thick fingers slid home into her center and she bucked, jerking from the pulsing pressure directly against her G-spot. A gasp caught on her lips. It came out as a sigh when he started a swift rhythm that delved deep, while he worked her clit with his thumb.

So much of the picture was wrong. Her toes wiggled, tensing, as she desperately tried to open her legs farther for his rough, punishing examination. So. Good. So. Wrong. With her arms tied behind her back the sharp pinch of her shoulders deepened into pain while she rode his fingers. His breath was hot on her neck, mutters of encouragement caressing her sensitive, dewy flesh. Every inch she strained made it worse as his fingers stretched her, the tension just on the verge of being too much for her to handle. Breaths sawed in and out of her lungs, burning, twisting into small cries while she imagined Hank's eyes glued to her glistening pussy as another man fucked her into oblivion.

"Do...you...like...the...show...baby?" she panted, arching her back so the stranger's fingers pressed at just the right angle, making her writhe while her inner walls clenched tight. "Is it... good...for you?"

"I love the way he fucks you, babe. You're so flushed and hot. I want my mouth on your nipples, my teeth teasing them until your breasts are red from my roughness. You like that, huh? What I wouldn't do to pull over this cab into a dark alley..." Hank hissed in through his teeth and moaned as he applied the brakes a little too hard.

The jerky motion sent them both hurtling forward as she impaled herself on the stranger's digits at the same time that he stretched her with another finger. She bit her lip from the brunt of pain, a quick ache that twined up her spine as her inner walls pulsed, fluttering around the invasion.

"So warm. So wet." The stranger laughed again. "Let's see how your mouth feels against my cock. Will it be as delightful as your cunt on my hand?"

Before she could reply he snatched a handful of her hair in

his tight fist and she jerked back on impulse, igniting a fire across her scalp. He twirled her long auburn hair around his fist—once, twice. She wet her lips, still riding her high of ecstasy because he never stopped fucking her with his fingers. There wasn't time to catch a thought before her awareness was shattered, flitting in a million different directions.

"I want you to come, screaming, while your mouth is sealed around my shaft."

With the explicit directive whispered against the tip of her ear, he wrenched her down until her open mouth was pressed down on his freed erection. Somehow he'd undone his pants and she hadn't noticed, too focused on his fingers inside her cunt. But now there was no denying the weighty, throbbing press of him on the back of her throat. She tried to swallow past the musky, throbbing taste of him. Not enough air, not enough space. He was everywhere, filling her to the brim as she struggled to take him inside her body.

He bucked his hips and groaned while she experimentally slid her tongue down his shaft. A shock twanged through her muscles when she realized his cock listed slightly to the left, unlike Hank, who was a straight shot. The stranger's shaft eased down the back of her throat with the force of his timed thrust upward, familiar yet so different. Anna fought back the urge to choke, throat muscles constricted. A cry hurtled up to her lips as the strange man circled her clit with his thumb. No escape. The cab surged through the darkness somewhere in the city and she couldn't deny that the possibility of someone seeing their odd tryst made the wicked surprise all the more of a turn-on.

"I can feel her pussy clenching my fingers, Hank. She's close. Gonna come all over me soon." The stranger spoke, breathless, straining while he used his grip on her hair to keep her head bobbing on his cock.

Anna's lips tingled, cunt pulsing from the tense ecstasy that was flowing outward into every atom of her being. Her limbs thrashed against her bonds. She saw a brief flash of light at the edge of her blindfold, while a complete stranger shoved his cock against the back of her throat before withdrawing in an edgy dance that left her on the brink of losing oxygen. The purr of the cab and Hank's soft swearing buffered the first wave of orgasm as she struggled to ride it out. All of her choice—gone—which only made her hotter, an edge that flushed her skin and made her inner muscles clamp down hard on the stranger's fingers. He thrust his cock up into her mouth in short, quick bursts that made her moan.

Hank pulled out of a lane and into another, making Anna slide across the seats, only steadied by the man's trembling grip in her hair. Beneath the sluggish afterglow and mottled thoughts, Anna struggled to keep up with his pace. His hip movements were erratic, saliva teasing her lips while she tried her best not to drag her teeth down his bobbing, large shaft. When his fingers eased out of her, she clenched down immediately, as if her body was dying to have him back inside. But his free hand was already pawing at her loose trench coat. His hot, calloused palm scraped across her nipple until he had a large handful of her breast. He squeezed until she squirmed, practically in the stranger's lap because of Hank's wild driving.

"Damn. Anyone ever tell you you're amazing at using your mouth?" The stranger's words whooshed out, his fingers spasming against the back of Anna's scalp and pinching her hair harder. His slick fingers clamped over her other breast hard enough to brand or bruise until she shuddered from the intense, intimate contact.

"I tell her that every night," Hank commented from the front.

"Mmm, you have a good teacher." The stranger slapped her

breast with his open palm as she sucked in air through her nose. When he pinched her nipple, she did him one better and swirled her tongue over the head of his cock before he had time to push her farther down.

"Christ."

He arched as the silky fabric teased over her eyelids and the exterior rush of city life was broken up by her determination to make the thankless stranger in her mouth come like a geyser. A litany of curses streamed from his lips. Meanwhile his hand roved over and mauled her breasts as if they were the most amazing things he'd ever touched in his life. Starbursts shot out from behind her eyelids, lungs heaving, trembling to keep up without the use of her arms while cool air kissed her slick pussy. The spreader bar slapped against the base of the seat. Hank kept whistling some random tune while she waited on the edge of a yawning precipice for the stranger to spurt his seed into her ready mouth.

The mere thought of it made her grind down uselessly into the seat, the friction blocked by her coat. Either way, his energy excited every bit of her until she was practically purring.

"Close, aw, close, baby." The stranger's cock throbbed in the back of her mouth, his fingers almost going limp in her hair before his grip tightened to the point where she sensed the sting of tears behind her eyelids. Her lips buzzed from friction, her thighs clenched tight with anticipation while a bead of sweat teased down the nape of her neck.

Close.

Almost there.

Two. More. Seconds.

Payoff.

WHAT HAPPENS IN VEGAS...

Tim Rudolph

Sometimes guys just want to get off.

Okay, Pinocchio, tell us another one. Truth is, guys *need* to get off. It's our *raison d'être*, which is a fancy way of saying that we're fools for our tools. We see a good-looking biscuit sitting on a plate, we're not happy until we smother it in gravy. It's a terrible analogy, but you get the idea.

And that's the great failing of my gender: Where girls just want to have fun, guys just want to have hot, sticky sex with Jessica Alba on the rec room pool table—while our girlfriends whip us up a postcoital soufflé. Or some other dick-centric variation on the theme. Call it the curse of the Y chromosome, but there it is.

But in every deck of cards there are always a couple of jokers. Some of us—okay, me—get our clocks wound from delayed gratification. I know that isn't very fashionable to admit, but I've never been a slave to fashion. That doesn't mean I'm not a big fan of other forms of indentured servitude.

For instance. I've been kneeling on this nasty bedspread in this skanky, pay-by-the-hour Las Vegas motel room for nearly an hour, waiting, waiting. You'd think that having my eyes taped over with ten-dollar poker chips and my bandana-bound wrists crisscrossed behind my back would cool this boy's ardor, wouldn't you? Oh, and did I mention the rubber phallus lodged in my mouth, or the braided-leather choke collar looped menacingly around my neck?

How pathetic, right? How disgusting. How humiliating.

Says you.

Says me: It's everything I could wish for.

But I'm not really traveling down this dark and twisted road alone, am I? Meet Bob, the unassuming corporate accountant, and his sugar-frosted wife Suzy, a popular orthodontist. It's their tenth anniversary, and we're here trying to re-create their wedding night, wherein the newlyweds recruited a downtown street hustler named "Vic" and, by all accounts, got every nickel's worth of satisfaction for the two bills they spent on him.

So how did we meet, and who the hell am I? That's easy. I've delivered Mr. and Mrs. Lowery's mail to their sedate, manicured suburban home in Rocklin, California for years. One day I happened to be leafing through their *Swingers Monthly* magazine in my mail truck (yes, we're all snoops) when I was startled by an insistent tap on my shoulder. Well, one thing led to another, and before long I was confessing to Bob how much I enjoyed playing the groveling manservant with other like-minded debauchees.

"Well, this calls for a road trip!" Suzy exclaimed after we'd exchanged pleasantries and Bob had filled her in on my "naughty nature," as he called it.

Suzy. She's got the legs of a Vegas showgirl coupled with a

showstopping backside that draws more double takes than Dolly Parton's tatas. That's her pacing the threadbare, gunk-stained carpet, working herself into a libidinous lather. When she gets like this, Bob claims, she can melt the ice in your drink with the heat from her cunt. Physics! Who knew?

What I *do* know is that there is a Live Nude Girl working the room, and she's thrown her mind right into the gutter. I mean, why else would we be shacked up in this raucous dump? Doors slam. Walls thump. Booze-fueled shouts echo down the dingy hallway. But this is the anniversary present that Suzy asked for, this cut-rate ambience, nasty as a razor nick.

Hey, every ten years, knock yourself out. Get your kink on. You might even enroll a pasty-white mail carrier to do your bidding.

Bob is certainly game. When last I saw him he was sitting naked on a straight-backed chair, idly stroking his cock while he watched Suzy undress me, then bind me, then blind me. (The rubber sex toy that I've been forced to suck on was his idea, the deviant bastard). Bob's not exactly a party animal, being a numbers guy and all. But he's no reluctant cuckold, either. He assured me that he would be happy to sit this one out because, well, he likes watching his wife get nasty with relative strangers.

"It keeps the old coffee percolating," he confided, winking lecherously. Marriage counselors, take note.

Okay. Wonderful. But one man's pleasure is another man's what-the-fuck. I continue to kneel, my legs cramping, my clean-shaven cock angry with razor burn. Christ, how much longer? The windowless room is hot like an oven and reeks of animals in rut and unfiltered Camels. But because I have no point of reference, it's easy to imagine that I'm in an underground tomb in decadent Rome, where I've been served up as a slavish trophy for some victorious, horny gladiator. My cock stirs at the thought.

Finally someone breaks the suspense. It's Bob, cracking open another Coors, the carbonated *phishh* so close that it tickles my nose. Lucky hubby has himself a ringside seat.

And then I feel the mattress give behind me, and I'm enveloped by the heady aroma of jasmine perfume. Suzy! She playfully tugs on my ears like I'm her housebroken puppy and says into one of them, "It's not nice to read other people's mail, Philip." She has the lilting, come-hither voice of a phone-sex operator, but lust has abraded it like sandpaper. "So I think I'll just have to go all postal on your ass. You don't mind, do you?"

"Mmphh" is all I can manage. But despite my discomfort—or maybe because of it—my cock continues to swell in anticipation. In anticipation of what, only the anniversary girl knows for sure.

"What's the matter," Suzy asks, laughing at my pained expression. "Cock got your tongue?"

This strikes Bob as hilarious; I can hear his high-pitched laughter catch in his throat, as though he's watching Sinbad crack jokes while he leans back in his chair, masturbating.

"Here," Suzy says. "Let's take that filthy thing out of your mouth—you wouldn't *believe* where it's been. Besides, there are other ways we can play."

So now it begins, I think. The dirty dentist has my punishment all mapped out. And she has a rapt audience of one who eggs her on by whispering sweet pornographic nothings from his bedside perch. Maybe these people are disciples of Sade. Maybe they're all about means to an end. Their means, my end.

"Beer," I say through numbed lips after Suzy uncorks the dildo from my mouth. My throat is as dry as the fake desert out by our rental car. "Please. Just a swallow."

Suzy jerks on my choker with surprising force, testing my gag reflex. "I like you better when you don't talk so much," she says. "Understand?"

But just as quickly she goes all Good Witch on me by holding a can of ice-cold beer to my lips. Oh, sweet nectar! Then she palms my balls in her creamy hand like they're delicate quail eggs, and part of me wants to believe that the worst is over. Maybe this whole production was just a warm-up act to see if I'd make an obedient plaything.

Yes! Maybe next time we'll do it up right at the Aladdin. Silk sheets. Room service. Jacuzzis!

"Well, my work is done here," I say, chirping like a goddamned canary in the jaws of a cat. "So feel free to cut me loose whenever you want. It's been fun, though."

Nobody says a word, but I can hear the bedsprings groan as Bob climbs up to get closer to the action. I imagine him and Suzy exchanging the knowing looks of the long-and-happily married and nodding conspiratorially. Then Suzy grabs a hank of my hair and snaps my head back.

"What part of 'no talking' didn't you understand? Dirty little fuck toys like you should be seen and not heard." To get more purchase, she winds the free end of the choker around my neck, doubling my agony. My thighs quiver in defeat, and I don't resist when she forces my head back down and plants my face on a musty pillow.

Okay. Deep breath. Time to reevaluate. I've played this role of Nancy Boy before. Face down, ass up. Submissive in every way. I can do this. I *want* to do this. Besides, in Vegas the house always wins, and Bob and Suzy—the dealer and the pit boss—are sitting on twenty-one.

"Perfect," Bob says, so close that I can smell his dime-store aftershave and hear the friction of his hand gliding over his cock.

"Not quite," Suzy says. "Aren't you forgetting the ring?"

The ring? What is *that*, some sort of sentimental keepsake celebrating their decennial? Because if it's not—

"Daddy's been shopping at the dirty bookstore again," Suzy says, laughing like a villain in a cartoon. "And I think it's just your size."

She shamelessly gropes my hairless cock and I'm thinking: *Oh fuck. The freaky degenerates are going to put my dick in a sling while I'm trussed up like a Thanksgiving turkey. Then they're going to take me for a joyride down BDSM Boulevard, where they'll probably do some terribly scurrilous things to me. Things that will turn me into a mewling slut who begs for more.*

Oh my god...Can it get any better?

Yes. But only if it gets worse.

The pretty practicing dentist tells me that this might pinch a little, and without warning she takes the slack out of my balls with one hand while the other gingerly works a narrow elastic cock ring over them until it grips the base of my shaft. Jesus Christ, my nut sac! I wince. I grunt. Tears come to my eyes. Now my balls are squished together like two peas in a perverted pod. I dig my fingernails into my palms, anticipating more pain, but it's the constriction that's killing me: The bitch has left me with a raging hard-on *and* a serious case of blue balls.

So why am I grinning like a shitfaced jack-o'-lantern?

"You like that, don't you, slutboy?"

I gasp, unable to answer—I hadn't expected such a hedonistic rush. I almost hate myself for being such a spineless church mouse, but I can't suppress my groans of gratitude.

"Yes," I finally manage to whisper. "I like it. Very much."

"And you'll do anything I ask, won't you?"

"Anything. Everything."

I feel her weight shift, and before I know it she's straddling my back and pulling hard on the choker. It hurts, but the way her sumptuous ass spreads indecently across my skin soothes and excites me. I can feel Suzy's arousal mount as well as she wantonly gyrates her pussy against my spine, smearing it with her juices.

It feels like the walls of the airless room are closing in. Now it's as steamy as a jungle hut and redolent of musk, making me half-crazy with lust. But Bob and Suzy, the wicked pirates who've hijacked my booty, have conspired to leave my aching cock in a state of rigid agitation by cutting my "boys" off at the pass. What they've done is so unspeakably cruel, so punishing, that my cock responds by weeping a drop of precome. Go figure.

"You know, Philip," Suzy says, panting huskily, "they say that every orgasm is like a little death." She smushes her tits against my back then sticks her tongue in my ear. "Ever had a near-death experience while jacking off? You know, where you get off just before you *kick* off? I understand that it's quite something."

"I'm not sure I..."

"Don't answer and don't argue." She two-fists the choker, then gives it a vicious twist, and I feel myself getting light-headed, like I'm sucking helium.

"Ride 'em cowgirl!" Bob hoots. But he wants to write his own salacious chapter to this bawdy novelette. "Two's company, three's an orgy," he says, chortling like a man who's about to lose his mind.

Yeah, well so much for sitting this one out. In a surprisingly athletic move he scooches under my upraised ass and takes my pulsing purple cockhead into his mouth, where he rolls it around on his tongue like a gumdrop. The sensation is shocking, thrilling, exquisitely depraved—the mild-mannered accountant has my number down cold.

But it's his wife who's the real sex maniac. Suzy's a hard-charging dynamo consumed with prurient behavior, and I can tell that she's caught up in Bob's down-and-dirty cock play by the way she rears back on the choker and rides me like I'm one of those barroom mechanical bulls.

"Fuck him, honey!" she says, digging her heels into my thighs. "Tickle his balls! Lick his asshole!"

Bob-the-party-crasher doesn't need any goading. He spits on my cock, then rolls it between his hands before taking the length of it to the back of his throat. Smutty lad! He's already got my sperm boiling, but now he ups the ante by worming his stubby finger into my asshole and rummaging around for my prostate.

"Christ, I need to come," I whimper, sounding like a school kid who's had his lunch money stolen.

Suzy laughs. "Don't we all? What do you think, husband? Does our fuck toy deserve his reward?"

But instead of showing mercy she cinches the choker up so tight that it bites into my windpipe. Okay, now I *really* can't breathe. At all! Panic sets in, but it soon gets displaced by a strange, suffusing calm. It's like I'm a South Seas pearl diver down too long without air, but past the point of caring whether I ever resurface. Big Bad Death? Big fucking deal. Bring it.

"He's coming!"

It's Bob, sounding like he's just hit the jackpot. Suzy immediately lets up on the choker, and I feel my lungs inflate like happy birthday balloons. Then her slender fingers partner up with Bob's, and while he swiftly rolls the cock ring off of my balls, she grips my shaft just under the head and jerks it like a woman trying to resurrect the dead. Everything gets lost except for the moment, but the moment obliterates me. The orgasm breaks over my head like a hundred-foot wave, and I come so hard that Suzy yelps with delight when I uncoil a rope of pent-up jizz that pools then quickly melts into the fucked-up, fucked-over bedspread.

Whew. Emission accomplished. Annihilation averted.

Ah, but this is Sin City, where vice is on call 24/7. In this town there really is no rest for the wicked. I've seen Bob and Suzy's satchel of toys—cuffs, plugs, clamps, gags—so I know that we're just getting started.

But do I look concerned? Am I wearing a poor-me frowny face? Not a chance. Because the postman always delivers, and he's brought a little something-something for the celebrating couple. It's nothing fancy. It doesn't come with ribbons and bows. It's just a little get-acquainted game he likes to call Return to Sender.

And it starts right now.

THE THUG

Sommer Marsden

"Boss said to keep you on ice in here." He dumped me in the claw-footed tub with a soft grunt. I have to hand it to him—he put his hand beneath my head to keep me from rapping it on the porcelain.

Then he sat back on his haunches and studied me. Tall and broad in a pin-striped suit and a fedora that had seen better days, he was handsome in a thuggish kind of way. The darkness in his brown eyes sent a chill through me.

He pushed my wavy bangs back into place, restoring my hairdo to pristine pin curls. I'd have thanked him but for the strip of duct tape over my lips.

"I'm only doing what the big boss wants, doll face."

Doll face. I shivered again. I imagined the big strapping body beneath that suit. The scars from a life spent wild.

"It's not necessarily what I want to do, see?"

I nodded vigorously. My best bet was to go along with whatever he said. His tie was askew slightly and some particular part of me wished I could straighten it.

He reached out slowly as if I would—as if I *could*—bite him, and stroked the sticky tape over my mouth. I felt a pulsing rush of blood in my pussy, a swollen kind of want in my clit. I shut my eyes briefly and tried to ignore the feel of my nipples going tight in my bra.

I shifted my wrists but the rough rope bit deep into my skin. I flexed my fingers to keep the blood flowing. I tried to wriggle my ankles in their hemp bonds, but only managed to make my arousal worse and twist my back-seam stockings around my legs.

"I could be persuaded, though. I could maybe accidentally let you go if you were to...do me a service."

His fingers smelled of the unfiltered cigarettes he'd been smoking since he nabbed me on my walk home from work, tied me up and dropped me in the backseat of his car, demanding I be quiet or I'd "be sorry."

The dress was hiked up around my hips and something was itching, which made my nose begin to itch. But I couldn't do anything with my hands bound and the sensation was starting to drive me mad.

I nodded. I'd do it. Anything. Whatever he wanted.

He grinned at me. His first true smile. It made him look less thuggish, but not a lot.

"Glad to hear it, doll face. Good to know some old-fashioned reason still works. I think you might even like the favor you're about to do for me. At least I hope you will."

He got me up on my knees in the tub, my belly pressing the porcelain. It was cold even through my navy-blue polka-dotted dress. I found myself wishing he'd take my dress off me, but I pushed the thought away. I watched him open his belt and then his pants. He didn't even have to fish around in his striped blue boxers for his cock. There it was, standing at attention, the tip flushed and shiny with urgency.

He looked me in the eye and there was that flash again, that darkness in his gaze that set off something deep inside me. "I'm going to pull that piece of tape off, okay? Don't get it in your crazy little head to do anything rash. Do you hear me?"

I nodded. My heart pounded and I wiggled my wrist again and felt my pulse beating crazy and heavy beneath my bonds. He pulled the tape off and I sucked in a great breath of air.

"I'll do whatever you want," I said. "Please."

He smiled, taking my face in his hand, running his thumb up my jawline. "You look like a smart dame. I'll trust you not to bite." Then he leaned in and tapped my lower lip with his cock. He smelled of tobacco, cotton and a musky cologne.

I shut my eyes and sucked his tip into my mouth. He pulled free and tapped my lip again. "Baby blues open," he said. He moved back enough for me to see my bright red lipstick ringing his cock. "See what pretty marks you leave."

Before I could reply he pushed his cock back in my mouth. I dragged my lips along his silken sheath, feeling the tip brush the back of my throat. My eyes watered slightly and I shivered. He chuckled and pushed a hand down into the bodice of my dress. He slid his fingers past the grayish blue silk brassiere I wore and pinched my nipple hard.

Conversationally, he said, "There's this stripper at this joint we go to, she rouges her nipples. Ever thought about rouging your nipples, doll face?"

I shook my head even as I tried to deep-throat him. I couldn't quite get to the root of his cock but I seemed to get points for effort because he sighed and gently stroked my hair.

"How about we rouge your nipples then? I might be inclined to untie your wrists for that."

I nodded vigorously, realizing as soon as he said it how terribly the rope was irritating my wrists. The bruiser attempted to unbutton the buttons on my bodice but abandoned his efforts after two failed attempts.

I moaned, moving my wrists restlessly against the edge of the tub to remind him.

"Patience, sweetheart. Patience is a virtue. Didn't they tell you that in school?" He stepped back, cock painted brightly with my lipstick. Then he took his fedora off and hung it on a wall hook. He opened the medicine cabinet and rummaged around. "Maybe the boss's missus has some in here. You never know what you'll find in these things. Dames keep all kinds of shi—sorry. All kinds of things in medicine cabinets."

He pulled out a blue makeup case and unzipped it, producing a small round compact. He flipped it open. "This rouge?"

He tilted it toward me and I looked. Cream rouge in a shade of rose. I nodded.

"You can speak, you know." He pointed at me. "You just can't scream. You scream and things could get rough."

"It's rouge," I confirmed.

He set the case down and nodded to my wrists. "Put them up."

I did as he said, my body showing a fine tremor from the adrenaline. He produced a pocketknife and began to saw at the rope that bound me. My skin emerged, tattooed with fine marks from the hemp. Pink and achy and shiny.

The thug surprised me by leaning in and kissing my wrists just above my pulse. "To make 'em feel better," he grumbled. Then he nodded to my dress. "Undo those buttons. Pull out those tits."

I bristled at his blunt language but did as he said. My fingers trembled as I undid the pearlescent buttons and then I pulled my bra cups down to expose my breasts. My knees ached dully from kneeling in the tub.

He squatted down and opened the small compact. "Remember, no screaming, no biting. And I'll be real nice to you."

I heard myself exhale. It was a stuttery breath. "I will. I promise."

He coated his thick fingertip in rouge and began to paint it on my nipple and the areola. I watched that pale pink flesh pucker and go tight beneath his touch. I moaned before I could catch myself. His dark eyes went to my face, and I felt naked beneath that brazen gaze.

"I'm going to assume the boss man wants you to play with. But I think I'll risk getting snuffed out to play with you myself."

He got more rouge and moved to the other nipple, stroking it, covering it in rosy pink. I clutched the edge of the tub to keep myself steady—and to repress my sudden urge to touch him of my own volition. I was supposed to be scared of the thug.

When both my nipples were painted fetching pink, he dropped to his knees and kissed me. I stiffened at first, tasting cigarettes on his tongue and wondering what kind of violence such a big man was capable of. Then he was stroking my freshly rouged nipples and kissing me and I let myself get lost in it. How gentle he could be. I sighed into his mouth before I could stop myself.

He laughed. "Not such a scary guy when I want to be nice, now am I?"

I shook my head, remaining mute.

"If I untie those delicate ankles of yours will you behave while I take off your shoes? And your hosiery? And your delicates?" he asked, his voice growing gruff as he spoke.

I nodded. "I promise. Anything," I said.

He lifted me out of the tub and carried me to a small room

with a sofa and a desk—someone's office. He set me on the sofa and put my feet in his lap, slowly but surely unwinding my ankles. He didn't use the knife this time but instead showed patience at undoing his own handiwork.

When the rope was puddled by his leg he got up and pulled me to my feet. "Arms up."

I put my arms up like a child and allowed him to pull my dress over my head and off. Next he unhooked my bra and dropped it at my feet. "I thought you were all tied up in my rope." He smiled and I realized it was a crooked smile, almost likeable. Handsome. Almost. "But you're much more bound by the stuff under your dress than by anything I supplied." He removed one spectator pump at a time.

I felt my cheeks turn as pink as my nipples when he unhooked my hose from my garter belt. Surprisingly, he knew how to roll them down properly so they wouldn't snag and could be stored. I felt myself go wet between the legs at the realization. His face was so near my underpants his breath penetrated the silk. The humidity of every exhalation was intoxicating.

I watched, fascinated, as he removed my garter belt and then my panties. I was bare before him.

"You're much prettier out of all those things than you are in them, doll face."

I could only nod.

"Spread your legs."

I spread my legs and with two big fingers he parted my nether lips. Then: "You're so pink down here you don't need any rouge." Then he pushed a finger inside me. I cried out little. He said, "And you're wet, too. Did I make you wet, sweetheart?"

I nodded.

"Good to know." He didn't say any more. He just leaned in and brushed his lips over my clitoris. He pushed his tongue into my slit as his big, heavy hands held on to my upper thighs. He kept me right on the edge to the point where I began to whimper.

"Oh, does my captive want to come?" he whispered.

I found my voice then. Maybe it had been unveiled by him removing all my restrictive clothes. "Yes," I said softly, my voice watery.

"Then come," he said, latching on to me, sucking harder and faster. His fingers drove into me over and over again and I found myself clutching his broad shoulders, still sheathed in his pin-striped jacket. I came, saying nothing but "Oh" over and over again.

He grabbed me and stood, moving toward the desk. Then he bent me over, put my arms across the blotter and took my hips in his hands. I arched back, shameless and helpless to deny that I wanted this. I did my best to beckon with my body. Not that I had to.

He hissed as he entered me. Just the tip at first. He made me wriggle and beg without begging. I could still feel blood thumping and rushing in my wrists and my ankles where he'd had me bound.

"I decided I wanted you for myself," he grunted.

I came.

"All for myself. Fuck the big boss."

He slammed into me, thrusting so hard my hip bones hit the edge of the desk. He pulled out of me and picked me up, laying me on my back, spreading me wide. His eyes ate me up. His gaze felt almost tangible. He parted my legs, hauled me forward so my bottom was on the lip of the desk and drove into me. "I want to see your pretty face when I come all over your pretty pale skin."

I gasped again, not just from his words but from his thumb,

which he pressed relentlessly against my clitoris as he thrust deeper and deeper still.

"I love what that pretty mouth of yours does when you gasp. I love what that pretty mouth of yours does on my dick," he said.

I moaned.

"I love all the pretty things about the pretty dame," he said gruffly. Then he laughed.

He made a sound—a simple animal sound—that told me he was about to come. I pushed my legs up a little higher to get him deeper. He rubbed my clitoris and when he said, "Christ," I came. Knowing he was right there.

He stayed in me long enough to feel my pussy milk at him and then he pulled free and shot his come all over my belly, using his fingers to rub it into my skin and paint it around my belly button.

He grinned at me. My thug.

"So there was your noir movie, *doll face*. What's next? Can I be big boss next time if we do noir again?"

I was shivering and Mike pulled me close, wrapping his arms around me to warm me. He'd taken the throw blanket off the back of his office sofa to set the scene.

"Not noir again. Sci-fi," I said, teeth clacking lightly.

"Oooh," he said, pulling a sweater from the closet by the sofa. "Can we have a scenario where I have more than one cock?"

I snorted. "We'll see. I'll have to think it over."

"Whatever you want, doll face," he said, laughing.

"Good thug," I said, kissing him.

HOUSEWARMING THE CRAFTSMAN

Daddy X

Tom and Ellen found the old two-story house tucked way at the top of the canyon. Just perfect for entertaining. No neighbors to hear any screams. Looking beneath a few cosmetic concerns like dust, dirt, broken windows and detritus, they came to believe it was solid and had been designed by one of the greats. Tom asked Ellen what she thought.

"Bigger than the ones you see in ordinary neighborhoods," she said.

"Nicer too," the agent Doris added. "In architecture school, they'd call it a Craftsman, American Arts and Crafts period. Early nineteen hundreds."

"Just look at that banister," said Ellen. "Those little openwork diamonds, hand-carved through the tops and bottoms of every upright post."

"Must have been *some* artist to come up with that," said Doris. "You can't even buy that quarter-sawn oak anymore."

"We'll take it," said Tom. "You say it's available for back taxes?"

"Yes," said the agent. "Down payment today, we'll expedite escrow. You'll be in by the end of next week."

Considering Tom's career in construction, they figured on doing most of the work themselves. Issues with the foundation and plumbing persisted, and the old coal burner had to be replaced, but the major effort would be spent on interior plaster and woodwork. Tom's business had grown to a point where he could delegate some duties. He turned authority over to a few trusted foremen to spend more time with Ellen while they were still young enough to share their good fortune.

Hard at it one day, Tom stopped for a drink.

Ellen had taken the staircase upon herself, starting with the banister. Dressed in little khaki shorts and T-shirt, her long legs straddled the rail, one foot solid on a lower step. She ran a square of sandpaper up and down in front of her, smoothing the wood to perfection.

Feeling wiseass, Tom cracked, "A little penis envy over there?"

"What's that?" she answered, drawn from her focus.

"You look like that's a massive brown cock, and you're masturbating."

"Hah! You nasty you," said Ellen, realizing the image she presented. "Hadn't thought of that," she giggled.

"Good thing it's just us. You're giving me a hard—"

"I can imagine what you're thinking. Pervert."

"Can you?" Tom teased. "What am I imagining?"

"Never know with you."

"Did the...ahem...the equipment," he said, "make it here yet?"

"Tom."

"Yes?"

"What are you thinking?"

"So? What's here?"

"I didn't—I didn't think we—"

"Would get the chance?"

"We *have* been busy," she said.

"There's always time for play."

Ellen and Tom had christened the place the night they moved in, making love on an air mattress on the floor. Whenever they had the time, energy and inclination, they did all the things lovers do with each other, weaving hands, mouths, cock and cunt together, embracing that sense of togetherness every couple needs.

But they hadn't yet had sex. Not *real* sex. They'd had equal exchanges of affection. They'd had sessions combining love, companionship and understanding. They'd sure fucked.

But no, not *that* kind of sex. Not yet.

"Stop being silly, Tom. Now you've got me going, you fuck-stick."

"What's 'got you going' supposed to mean?"

Ellen grinned, a hint of the devil in her eyes. "Well, I already have something between my legs," she teased, angling her torso into a pelvic curl, rubbing her pussy up and down the recently sanded banister.

In a show of purpose, Tom stepped to the room used to store equipment. He rummaged through various tools and unpacked boxes. There should be something he could use. Yes, the Velcro straps. Long shears. That's all he'd need. This time.

Back in the living room, he told Ellen, "Let me show you a trick to get inside those little diamonds in the uprights."

"Yeah," she said, "rolling up the sandpaper doesn't—"

"Well, it won't really matter if the inside of the holes are a little darker," said Tom. "It doesn't have to be perfect; it's an antique. Just rough it up so the varnish sticks."

"Okay, show me," she said, sitting up. One leg still over the rail.

Tom scaled a few steps. "Okay—thread this through a diamond hole here," he said, running a Velcro strap through an oaken strut above her. "Here, hold this end."

"Let's see. Like this?" she said, leaning forward on the banister, concentrating on the process.

He mumbled.

"What?" she looked up. "Didn't hear that."

The distraction provided the seconds Tom needed. He flipped the Velcro around one wrist, then, in a flash, the other. "Gotcha!" he said.

While Ellen hesitated, flummoxed by the abruptness of her situation, Tom stretched her bare leg down a few steps, fastening the ankle to the bottom of a lower upright.

Ellen had the idea now, arms stretched along the banister, one foot tied at a lower step, the other free leg still over the rounded rail. No chance of falling off. "Oh you fucker!" she exclaimed. "I can't trust you?" Ellen tugged at her bonds to no avail. The foot on the stair held her balanced, crotch against the sensuous wood.

"Not when it comes to this," he said.

No longer in a hurry, Tom backed down the steps and sat in the living room. What a lovely apparition his wife made, fastened along a banister in T-shirt and shorts, bound at three points. Her pert breasts pulled the T-shirt tight on both sides of the banister. "And one more thing," he said.

Confusion rectified itself in Ellen's mind. Her throat turned gravelly, warm, knowing whatever happened after this point would stray pleasingly beyond her control. Beyond what she was taught. Beyond what a respectable woman should want or need. What was right. What was wrong. Tied to a banister, without a choice. "What now?" she groaned, heated, resigned.

Tom made his way back up the staircase. He tugged Ellen's T-shirt up to her shoulders, unsnapped her brassiere and slid it up above her breasts. It created an obscene look, one dusky-tipped cone of flesh hanging on each side of the rail, empty cups and bra strap bunched up with the shirt around her neck.

"God, you're beautiful," he said, crouching, fondling first the tit on his side, then tweaking the other through the banister posts.

"You always say those things when I'm tied up," she said with a bit of nostalgia.

Nostalgia wasn't the only sensation sweeping through Ellen's mind and body. Tom's caresses warmed her entire being. An involuntary press of her bothered cunt against the railing. Little pelvic tilts. A flush to her face. Those shorts that usually fit so loose, now hugged tight across her buttcheeks. When she let her entire weight down, the banister pressed uncomfortably against her crotch. Ellen found that if she held herself up a bit on the one grounded foot, the sensation could be adjusted, altered to be almost pleasant.

As it is whenever a man or woman places something between their legs.

Tom's admiring gropes found their way along Ellen's smooth little buttocks, fingers tickling along the center divide, pausing under the moist, unprotected area she held above the carved wood.

Ellen's asscheeks clenched. "Oh fuck, Tom. Don't do that. Not if you don't mean it," she moaned, eyes drooping.

"I mean it," he whispered.

Back in the living room, Tom brought out an iPhone. "Wait'll our friends see this."

Click.

"You *would* do that, wouldn't you?"

"You bet," he said. "Just wait for the housewarming. They'll *all* get an eyeful."

Tom flashed her the photo.

"Well, what if I don't want people seeing me like that?" Ellen asked, cheeks reddened.

"Fat chance," he retorted. "A show-off like you? You get off on it. It's that exhibitionist shame that turns you on."

Raising an eyebrow, Ellen turned to Tom. "Lots of talk from a guy getting his jollies watching his horny wife tied helpless."

"You better watch your mouth, you little slut."

Ellen rubbed a longer swath of banister with her crotch, directing her torso up the rail then down, the subtle rhythm further antagonizing her libido. "What will Daddy do if Mommy doesn't want to be quiet?" she asked singsong, wiggling her ass at the bottom of a curl, acting coy. "What's the big man gonna do? With his helpless little captive brunette?" She raised the untied leg to reveal a dark spot developing on the khaki.

"Do you really want to know?" Tom replied in mock annoyance. "Or do you want a surprise?"

"Could you give me a little of...both?"

"Oh, I'm gonna give you something, all right," Tom said, easing into the wordplay. "I'm going to run my cock up your little brown asshole."

Ellen came right back with, "Promises, promises. You can't even take my shorts off, not with me like this."

His double take gave him away.

"Uh-oh," she said. "Now I've done it, haven't I?"

Ellen wasn't sure how hard to push. Sure, she'd been tied up helpless before, genitals exposed, fucked far beyond what she would have allowed if not restrained. Successive orgasms in more volume, in more shapes, of greater screaming intensity than she could remember. More, in fact than she would have believed possible. Being unable to shut down the gropes and manipulations exposed her sexual triggers. Manipulations of her cunt, clit, asshole and mouth. Lubricated hands. With tongues. With vibrators, dildos, nipple clamps, butt plugs and feathers. And cocks. Always cocks. And sometimes a flail. Tom had always been worthy of her trust before. Yet it didn't stall the flurries of fear, those enticing flurries.

Tom grabbed the shears and marched to the stairs. "Yes, you little sass mouth," he blurted in exaggerated pomposity. "Prepare to be ass-fucked, woman! On your own living room banister."

"Oh god. Did you find the lube?"

"Lube?" he said incredulously. "What lube?"

"Come on, Tom," she said. "Don't dry-fuck me here. Please? Tom, don't. I'll be good."

"Too fucking late," he said. "You've turned me on, slut. And I'm not going through all those fucking boxes just to find your goddamn lube. Not with this hard-on you just gave me, you little cunt." He rubbed the front of his blue jeans, further enhancing the stirrings she'd begun. "Chrissakes, look at this thing."

"Oh!" she said. "Did Tommy's little wifey-poo get him all hot and bothered? Won't he let her down to do something about it? Big meanie won't even let her have any lube." She plumped her lower lip in a show of mock defiance.

"I'll be the one to say when and how I fuck you," he said, twisting his face into a phony sneer. "With lube or not."

This was the part of the game Ellen was never quite sure of. She didn't want to be rasp-fucked. Although she knew she could trust Tom, she couldn't be exactly sure how far, not when he got that wound up.

And she could see how his state was becoming, not only from

the bulge in his pants, but by his vacant, hypnotic stare. How healthy was he?

Ellen eyed the shears with a sensible skepticism, imagining the various things that could happen from this point. Would he cut her loose? Not a chance; it wouldn't do to cut the Velcro. He wasn't intending to do anything but intimidate her, she figured. She hoped.

"I can blow you if you climb the stairs," she said, hoping to ameliorate his passion somehow. "I'll turn my head like this and suck you off."

"That would work for starts," he replied, unzipping.

"Then what?"

"Already told you."

"My ass?"

"Open your mouth," he said. "Wide."

"Ahhh—"

"Now just keep it open," he said. "Like that. Keep it open. I'll dip in and out. Don't close down on me. I want you to keep open!"

"Ahhh...haa," she replied, increasingly aware of forbidden pleasures building between her legs.

Tom held the base of his cock in one hand, directing the tip over Ellen's lips, slowly tempting her, inserting it, then easing back.

Ellen couldn't resist her own reactions. Repeated mouthy reflexes activated her greedy maw involuntarily, her grasping lips trying to close around the bulb of Tom's jumpy cock, grabbing in vain at the velvety knob.

"Don't close, don't swallow," he said. "Let the saliva build. Keep your fucking mouth open, or I'm gonna fuck your ass right now."

"My shorts are on," she teased. "What about that?"

He grabbed the long shears then tugged at her waistband.

Ellen felt cold steel sliding down the crack of her ass.

Snip.

The industrial scissors made short work of the tiny shorts and undies all at once. Splayed fabric opened like a book, framing the tightest, roundest, cutest buttocks a guy ever had the privilege to stick a dick between.

"Oh fuck," she said. "My favorite work shorts!"

"Ruined now. Open your mouth."

Ellen's husband's cock resumed its probe, in and out of her parted lips. The shaft pressed farther in, gently folding her tongue against the back of her throat, allowing breath, but not allowing her to close her mouth. Her sense of shame had taken over her sense of judgment. Cheeks overflowed; drooling liquids ran around the hard muscle.

She sensed a hand under her neck. Was Tom collecting the dribbling spittle that dripped off her chin? "Ghaa. Ghaa haagg..."

The cock's exploration of her oral cavity became something of a reflexive challenge for Ellen. She wasn't greedily sucking at it like she would on an ordinary day; this certainly was no ordinary day. Each time Tom's cupped hand filled with drool and precome, she felt the touch of him, smearing the liquid between the cheeks of her spread ass, moistening her. A gently twisting fingertip slipped through the tough ring. She swayed her pelvis side to side, mashing her vulva across the top of the banister, directing it to her little bump as the soggy mound crossed and recrossed contours of the lengthwise column.

A thick middle finger explored deeper. Shoved in to the base, his big square row of knuckles forced her buttcheeks asunder, deforming the malleable globes.

"Umm...unnh," she moaned.

"Don't close your mouth. Don't swallow."

Finally satisfied that sufficient moisture existed to ease the way, Tom set his jeans aside, coated his dick with Ellen's spittle and swung a leg over the rail behind his wife. Nestled up close to her ass, his hard, leaky cock settled lengthwise into the fleshy divide.

"Now, baby," she moaned. "Fuck my ass now."

"Told you I would," said Tom, inserting his thumbs lengthwise into the crack. He spread her cheeks apart, exposing the tiny brown asterisk. "Relax," he said.

"Relax?" replied Ellen. "Up here?"

"You're not going anywhere," he assured her. "Nobody's falling."

Before the drool and jizz could dry, Tom pressed his cock against the hard, puckered muscle, massaging her sphincter with its tip, corralling sticky moisture to the point of insertion, where it would do the most good. He forged carefully on, encouraging her. "Open, my sweet. Open yourself to me. Bear down."

"Push," she sobbed. "Push, baby! Into your wanton wife's little pucker."

Tom pushed. Inch by soppy inch, he entered her darkest regions.

Ellen's elastic ring relaxed; her resistance gave way. "I'm ready," she muttered.

Now accustomed to his girth, she shuffled back against him, whimpering, impaling herself deeper and deeper on his cock, now at maximum hardness and length, fully relinquishing passage through her acquiescent ring.

Tom leaned forward over her sweaty back, saliva mixed with precome lubricating the way, wagging his lower torso slowly one side to the other, inching farther and farther into his wife's vast nether regions. He held himself above, not exerting that force, that power he had to keep in control. Not pounding her ass like a pile driver. Discipline. Discipline was needed in times like these.

Then Ellen was coming. Spouting profanities, sputtering emotive sequences reserved for lovers. No student of language could make any sense of the squeals, cries and excessive emanations echoing through the empty house. Wiggling her ass as much as her bindings allowed, Ellen forgot the meaning of demeanor, forgot the meaning of shame, forgot what it meant to be held captive without protection.

Tom followed her lead, his own orgasm welling up behind his ears then emptying into her quivering buns.

Throughout the months that followed, though Tom and Ellen looked forward to finishing the project so they could start throwing parties again, they made the best of the months spent working. It happened every now and then, sometimes several times a week. Sometimes they found themselves inspired by a tool, or a job that needed attention.

When it became necessary to replace the heavy crossbeam over the passageway from the parlor to the dining room, a small block and tackle was utilized. Sure enough—later that night—there was Ellen. Nude. Suspended, blindfolded, arms spread, hanging from the beam. Her stance divided the bulk of her weight between two short stools set a yard apart, rendering her exposed, vulnerable. Her slender torso was strung up at eye level with the very pulleys they'd employed to hoist the beam.

Ellen asked, "How long am I going to hang here?"

Never mind that Tom had unlimited access to her intimate parts. It wasn't Ellen's fault anymore. Ellen wasn't protected from his touches, or anybody's touches. It didn't matter that she'd always craved those touches, those debaucheries that had resulted in her reputation in college. Nympho Ellen, the insatiable slut who welcomed any and all advances from both men and women. Not her fault anymore. Out of her hands. Her hands were tied.

Tom spent much of that evening naked, rubbing up against his wife at will, kissing her, pinching nipples in clamps, teasing her unmercifully, penetrating her tender parts with fingers, tongue and various objects, eliciting moans and sighs with each caress. Later, after Ellen came down, they fucked themselves to a deep sleep, cuddled on the floor among the tools and sawdust.

The job was nearly done. Other than a few minor details, the major work was finally accomplished; it was high time for a celebration of sorts. Tom brought home some black leatherwork he'd designed for entertaining purposes.

Ellen asked, "What are those?"

"A couple of things I made up."

"What for?"

"Well, I bought the braided leather stock, took some measurements, added a couple of pulleys, and put 'em together."

"What kind of measurements?"

"Oh, nothing," he said. "The banister. The leather. You."

"What do you have in mind, Tom? What are you thinking?"

"Take off your clothes."

"Now?"

"Unless you have somewhere to go..."

"So—this is the big night?"

"Wait'll you see, honey," he said. "You won't believe how hot you'll be."

Once she'd undressed, Tom guided Ellen to the side of the stairs in the living room, having her back up against the newly finished rungs of the staircase. "Hold along the banister with your arms stretched out," he said. "They'll be slanted up and down."

"Like this?" Ellen reached out to her sides along the handrail, right arm high above the other on the bias.

"That's perfect."

Tom wound a single leather thong around each arm along the rail, creating a spiral pattern pressed into his wife's skin, taking care not to exert too much pressure, cutting off circulation. He continued wrapping the binding round and round her torso and staircase uprights, further supporting her weight, breasts displayed in enticing linear asymmetry. Ellen's desire-hardened nipples poked out, pinched among crisscrossing strips of black braided cord, contrasted against her pale skin.

"Step through these loops," he said, indicating her right leg.

"Okay."

He spread the straps evenly along Ellen's thigh, gathered them together in one bunch then hooked them to a pulley he'd fastened to the higher side of the banister. The mechanical affair pulled her thigh above her waist, knee rising, calf and foot dangling. Ellen's pussy lips parted. He pulled the other leg straight out along the bottom, parallel to the stairs, tying her off to the lower struts in another pattern, thus supporting the rest of her. His wife, legs wide apart, was attached to the staircase in a classic Art Deco running pose, as if a bound Nike could take to the air in one giant leap. *The doorbell rang.*

"They're here, baby."

"Good god," gasped Ellen. "How do I look?"

"Gorgeous, sweetheart," he pronounced, tweaking her nipples pink. "Just wait'll they see you."

"Everything ready?"

"Let's see," Tom thought out loud, noting objects neatly assembled on the coffee table. "Plenty of food and drinks. Vibrator, remote, lube, dildos, nipple clamps, flail, condoms. Surgical gloves, for the squeamish. Yep, everything's good. Oh, wait a minute." He fingered Ellen's swollen pussy, making sure droplets in her pubic hair glistened under the chandelier.

"Oh Tom," she sighed, nearly breathless. "Let them in... please."

Tom opened the door. "Hello, hello!" he turned back toward the house. "It's the Watsons, dear. Bill and Janet! Welcome, folks. Here, let me take your coats. Ellen's tied up right now."

A well-turned-out Janet Watson floated into the parlor, captivated by her hostess's naked body lashed to the staircase. "Ahh..." she said, "reminiscent of early Abramovic."

"Simply lovely," said Bill. "Happy housewarming, you two. Smells like cunt in here. Jesus, you've really done wonders with this place. Great living art, by the way."

"Thanks, Bill," said Tom. "It took lots of effort, but we think it's worth it. Ellen's raring to go."

"She looks so helpless and lonely up there," said Janet. "May I kiss her?"

"Sure, sure," said Tom. "She won't be alone long, so nuzzle yourself right in there. Try the wet spot. But Ellen's far from lonely. In fact, she's been looking forward to this since we bought the place. Can I get anyone a drink? Hors d'oeuvres?"

"Thank you," said Bill, nodding toward Ellen. "I'll take some of that."

"Of course," replied a cordial Tom. "Would you like to fondle her? Or would you rather slip her the schwanz? Condoms right there on the table. Now or later, whatever...but that's quite the hard-on you're sporting. Hey, look! Here come the Harpers! And there's the Kaminskys, right behind them. This looks to be a glorious evening."

MULTIPLE CHOICE

Emily Bingham

I wake up smiling. Every creaking joint and sore muscle flashes me back to a bed that isn't mine. That vague pain in my shoulders is a memory of my wrists tied to the headboard. The ache in my knees and the absolute necessity for coffee are pleasant reminders of the reasons I didn't get much sleep.

The tightness in my boxers forces me out of the daydream of sweaty bodies and entangled limbs, back to the present as I undertake the ritual of caffeine making. Watching the oily ground beans drenched in hot water brew, there's no harm in snaking a hand down the front of my body. Images in my head of last night have made me instantly erect. The problem is, once I get started it's difficult to stop.

Soon, I'm leaning against the counter, breathless, stroking myself and glad my housemate sleeps until noon. At least I hope he will today because I'm at the point where I can't let go of the momentum. The danger of being caught only forces me closer to release.

My mind flashes through a best-of compilation of sexiness. Heaving bodies, wet flesh, soft lips, hard cock. I'm a goner, coming in my kitchen before the coffee is ready. I clean up and caffeinate. It's time to focus; there are things to do today and being distracted while on a ladder just won't do.

Morning preparations complete, I brace myself for the outdoors. It's wet, dark, depressing—a typical winter in Oregon. That pleasant, sexy buzz melts away almost instantly. The cold months have a way of sapping the joy out of a person. To make things worse, while dragging the ladder out of hiding I notice something on the windshield of my car. A hit of rage gets my blood racing.

A parking ticket? Really?

As I get closer, I realize it couldn't be. Even the progressive city of Portland wouldn't be using purple paper to issue citations. Intrigued, I pick up my pace. The mystery is so great I want to extend the moment. I run a finger along the edge of the paper and then end the torment of not knowing by opening it.

Seven p.m. My place. Dress well.

It isn't signed but I have a good idea who left the note. My pulse is raised for more pleasant reasons now. Looking around, I wonder if I'm being watched. This thought somehow makes it hotter. I fold the paper and slide it into my front pocket, feeling an impossible heat radiating off of it. Suddenly I know exactly how I'm going to stay warm and motivated today. The sooner I finish, the sooner I can think about those six simple words. Gutters have never been cleaned with such intensity.

Later, soapy, slippery and hot in the shower, I'm tempted to jerk off again, but don't. I decide to delay the pleasure but regret the decision when faced with getting dressed. Even at half-mast, fitting my dick into the slick black pants is a struggle. It takes all my willpower to think of anything dull enough to make it possible to dress without this throbbing ache of need taking over. I zip up and sigh, one step closer to getting out the door.

Then I wonder, is it wise to be contemplating this? I'm not even positive who left the note. What if I get to her house and she's busy? She'll give me that look that says, *Fella, I think you're hot and all but I've got other plans*. But it *has* to be her words; it's not wishful thinking.

In dress pants, a button-down shirt, suit coat and shiny black shoes, I cut a pretty dapper figure. Nerves make it difficult to recall where to find my phone, keys and wallet but I eventually manage. Luckily, the autopilot section of my mind takes over, aiming me in the right direction while the rest of me plays over the possibilities of what could soon take place.

Pulling into a driveway on a dark street jerks me back to reality. This feels ominous, like the beginning of a cautionary tale: *Portland man, murdered by woman he met online. News at ten.* And yet the lust coursing through me opens the car door and guides me to the back of the house, through the noisy gate and into the total darkness of the backyard. I realize I've never seen her place in daylight.

Just before reaching to knock, I notice the bench to the right of the door, illuminated in the glow of the porch light. My name is written in feminine script on the note card attached to the paper bag. This makes me both more and less nervous, but at least I now know I'm in the right place.

My blood races, causing my hearing to go womb-like and become the only sound I hear. My body is betraying me, depriving me of one of my senses before she can.

The door is unlocked. Put what you find in the bag on your wrists and come inside.

Slipping this card in my pocket with the other note, I open the bag. I'm almost afraid to look. Whatever is inside feels small but heavy. In the darkness, I have no clue what it could be. I give it a tentative once-over with my fingers; it's something smooth with a furry edge and dangerously cold metal.

Holding my breath, I drop the bag to reveal a set of leather fur-lined restraints with metal rings on them. Not wanting to delay the moment any longer, I spread one open to wrap it around my wrist and the buttoned cuff of my shirt. It's strangely exciting, pulling it tight and cinching it off at the first position that feels comfortably snug. I repeat this on the other wrist, a little weak in the knees to realize how out of control this feels, being under her spell without having anything but written words for guidance.

I hesitate for a moment before pushing the door open and stepping inside. The warmth of the house hits me, calming my senses a bit. I'm not sure where to go or what to do now that I'm here. The next logical step is to remove my blazer, but when I go to do so the leather cuffs make that impossible. Before I can contemplate taking them off to slip out of the jacket, I hear the distinctive sound of heels clacking from the other room. The goose bumps are instantaneous.

Poking her head around the door frame, she looks me up and down. She raises her eyebrows in a way that leads to a dangerous grin. She must like what she sees.

"Do be a dear and join me."

It's my turn to take in the sight of her as she rotates on her stiletto heels to sway back to the living room. The back-seams of her stockings are impeccably straight, pointing like an arrow up the back of her thighs to the round of her ass. It wiggles, knowing I'm watching. She lures me in, forcing me to overcome my hesitation and follow her. There's an unspoken promise to those curves, accentuated as they are by the cinch of the corset that pulls in her waist. The bow tying all the lines together makes her look like a present I can't wait to unwrap. Except she's likely to make sure I'm wrapped up tight before allowing me the privilege of touching her. Luckily, she's worth the wait.

This room is better lit so that I can tell the furniture has been moved to the walls. At the center of the empty hardwood floor is a wooden chair. It doesn't take much imagination to know what comes next.

"Please, take a seat."

I do. The cold of the wood saps some of my heat and a chill runs up my spine. Folding my hands in my lap, I patiently watch her circle the chair. The drumming of her heels echoes like a threat until she stops behind me.

The first contact of her fingers tenderly resting on my back startles me. She caresses the tension out of my muscles, massaging at the places sore from my afternoon of manual labor. Her hands on my shoulders melt me into relaxing. She moves on to stroking my hair, making each follicle stand at attention, much like my dick is doing, nuzzling into my palms. With her watching, I know I shouldn't rub myself through the fabric of my pants, but I can't help it. She notices and tsks. Using my hair as a handle, she pulls my head back, forcing me to look at her.

"Handsy! We'll take care of that."

She walks around to the front of the chair. Kneeling, she places one hand on each of my thighs, parting them, and insinuates herself between my legs. Taking one of my wrists in each palm, she guides them behind the chair, holding them there. The weight of her chest on my crotch as she leans forward makes me groan. I want to grab hold of her, keep her close. No chance of that, however, as I hear a click behind me. Testing my bonds, I find she's trapped my hands together and to the chair.

She leans back to look at me deviously, fingers going for the clasp of my pants. My dick is freed from its confines and pops out to say hello. Her grin gets bigger. She doesn't touch me, just tucks the fabric of my fly to the sides, admiring from afar. Biting her lip, she rubs her crotch against the toe of my shoe, torturing me.

When I think she may take pity on me by stroking my dick, instead her hands reroute farther north to undo the first few buttons on my shirt. Using my shoulders for leverage, she stands and kisses along this newly exposed flesh. Chills again. I attempt words but instead come up with moans and heavy breathing.

Please is what I want to say. As in, *Please touch me, please, I want you.*

Before I can form words I'm distracted. She's raising her skirt to reveal that no panties are involved in her outfit, just a garter belt trapping the black contrast top of her soft nude stockings. Her fingers go to her clit, touching but not rubbing, teasing herself to tease me. Throwing one leg over my lap and stepping in closer, she brings her pussy dangerously close to the head of my cock.

She wouldn't dare, and yet the promise is there. She could do anything and I couldn't stop her. The sway of her hips is a hint of what could come later. She toys with the denial of touch and the cruelness of her closeness. Her eyes close and the movement of her fingers becomes more focused. With her head back, noises escape her throat, which make me throb at the sadism of her neglect.

"I'm ready for you," she growls while coming, or close to it. Her breathing is heavy. At first I think her words are directed at me, until a door down the hall opens. Footsteps get closer, however I can't see around her body to find out who else is in the house.

A feeling between dread and anticipation fills my every fiber as I try to crane my neck to see. She puts this attempt to an end by cradling my head with her free hand. This forces my face against the corset boning. My lips brush the landing strip of her pubic hair. A tentative exploration reveals that my tongue can't reach her flesh. I feel the ministrations of her fingers, and her gasps, but it's impossible to get too lost in the heat of the moment knowing a stranger is lurking behind me.

Her hand grasps my neck. Nails dig into my skin as she comes, her legs trembling on either side of my thigh. She steps back, slowly removing the fingers from the wet center of her to slide them into my mouth. My eager tongue is more than happy to help. Too soon, she pulls them away with a wet pop. Leaning down for a kiss, her hand is still in my hair, so that I'm unable to move away. The warmth of her tongue tickling mine makes me buck against the restraints.

Suddenly a second set of hands trace their way up my bound arms, feeling at the muscles there made moot by the leather cuffs. My body goes stiff with nerves. She straightens and leans over my head to kiss the person I can't see. I'm not even sure of the gender of this unseen guest, which makes things all the more mysteriously dangerous. It's cruel to listen to them touch and kiss, hands wrapped around one another with me in between but unable to participate.

"Please," I finally eke out, not sure what I mean but glad when they stop.

"Please what?" She gives me a look that lets me know she's perfectly aware of what I want. Her eyes flit up to the other person, giving them the come-hither head motion.

A second body joins her in my frame of vision. He's tall but burly. Messy hair falls in his eyes. The odd tangle of tattoos on his arms and the untucked shirt give him an air of carelessness. His eyes roam up and down my body, reminding me that I'm exposed. Again I experience that mix of shame and excitement.

"Hmm?" She's still waiting for me to use my words but I can't find any. I'm suddenly content to sit back and watch how this unfolds. Not that I have any other option. Her eyebrows rise, waiting for my response; when none appears, she gives up. Grabbing her friend, she kisses him deeply. Their hands are everywhere. Clothes come off.

His shirt goes first, revealing a wide, hairy chest and more tattoos. He returns the favor by unclasping her bra and tossing it aside, her generous breasts still cradled by the bust of the corset. Their chests touch and I wish I could feel either of them anywhere. They stand just out of the reach of my legs, but close enough I can hear the sound of their tongues and smell the lust between them.

A drop of moisture dribbles down my cock. The teasing is almost too much to take. I close my eyes against the ache of an erection getting no attention.

The sound of denim and a belt buckle hitting the floor snap me back into the moment. He's naked now, his sizable cock hard. Her hands are all over it. While she strokes its length, he moans and bucks against the rhythm of her movements, hoping to convince her to move at a faster pace. Instead she pushes him away, taking a fist of his chest hair and throwing him back on the couch. He laughs as we watch her step out of her skirt. She's clothed only in corset, stockings and heels now.

She kneels in front of him, taking his cock into her mouth, deep-throating him. His eyes roll back in his head in delight. I watch as she reaches for a condom that he isn't aware of yet. As he's losing himself to her sloppily bobbing him in and out of her mouth, she stops and stands. He groans, ready to complain until he sees what she holds. His face brightens.

Except she's walking away from him, lipstick a smeared mess, opening the condom and holding eye contact with me. Her friend and I exchange confused looks. He lies back, watching, touching himself, seeming content to wait. His hardness is a mirror image of mine, but he's allowed the pleasure I'm being denied. My brain is so lust addled I can't guess what she has in mind and I keep getting sidetracked watching the show he's putting on.

"You like to watch, don't you, dear boy?"

I nod, understanding now as I gaze up at her. Slowly, she finishes unbuttoning my shirt as he watches, rubbing himself, dick slick with her saliva. She lingers, legs close to me, fingers playing down my chest, mouth kissing my neck. My face drifts toward her, rubbing my cheek against hers to have some physical contact. She puts her lips near mine, asking without words if I would like access to them.

"Please?" I whisper; it seems to be the only word I remember. She fills that tiny space between the two of us and kisses me wetly, but only for the briefest moment. The taste of her mouth is the sweetness of her tongue and salt of his cock. Pulling away, she walks back to the couch.

She moves his hands away and deftly pushes the latex sheath over his hardness. Her pussy isn't far behind as she straddles him, purposefully angling their bodies so that I'm provided the perfect view of their sexes meeting. I sigh, struggling uselessly against the cuffs, wishing I could jerk off to this display. His cock spreads her open, her lips hugging his length each time she rises up and down over him. The speed of their thrusts, him lifting his hips to meet her, increases quickly. There's the slap of skin meeting again and again, until he lifts her off his lap and grips her waist to put her down on the couch.

The glare she gives him seems to express that she would be pissed off about the interruption if she weren't already so worked up. He laughs and flips her over so that her ass is in the air. Looking in my direction, he repositions her so that I can watch as he puts just the head of his dick into her. Teasing. She thrums at her clit with her fingers until she gets frustrated enough to back up against him, filling herself to moaning. I know her noises well enough to realize that she's coming. Holding on to the cushions of the couch, she thrusts back into him. Every muscle in her body is clenched. My cock twitches.

He follows her into bliss, grabbing her tight enough that she cries out, and he grunts while orgasming. As they recover, in a pile of naked body parts, I wonder if they've forgotten about me altogether. I make a pathetic noise to draw attention to myself. It works; they sit up and look at me. There are whispered conspiracies, then simultaneous evil smirks.

"You've been so good," she says. They stand and walk to me, tenderly rubbing one knee each. "As your reward you get to pick which one of us you'd like to suck that lovely cock of yours."

Looking up at their spent, sex-moistened bodies, I open my mouth to reply.

TYING THE KNOT

Rob Rosen

Ron, my fiancé—with T-minus-twenty some-odd hours and counting until we were officially hitched—rolled over, looked me right in the eye, and said, "I, um, love you, Ted."

I grinned and nodded. "I love you, too, Ron."

His nod mirrored my own. "I know. It's just, I love you, but I don't want to get married tomorrow."

My nodding promptly stopped. My grin promptly vanished. And I promptly reached over to his side of the bed and socked him one in the arm. "So not funny, Ron."

He rubbed his arm and frowned. "So not trying to be, Ted."

I sighed. "You're just having second thoughts, is all," I calmly explained. "That's completely natural. Cold feet, they call it."

He rolled over onto his back. "I had second thoughts all day, Ted. I'm now on to sevenths and eighths." He blinked. "No, scratch that, ninths."

To be honest, this was fairly par for the course for my husband-to-be. It took him a month to decide on the proper color of yellow for our bathroom. It wasn't until we painted it lemon that he upped and decided on canary. He also couldn't decide if we should lease or own our car. Sadly, I'm still taking the train to work. Still, this was our wedding he was talking about, not a Prius and certainly not a color swatch.

My sigh repeated. "How about sleeping on it, Ron? We can decide in the morning if we need to cancel the chapel, three hundred miles away, the reception hall, also three hundred miles away, and let the guests know not to come—all three hundred of them." Ironically, it was supposed to be two hundred, but Ron couldn't decide who *not* to invite, and so...well, you get the drift.

Again he nodded, downed a Xanax, and replied, "Okay, sure, hon. Sleep on it. Right." He again looked my way. "This is California, after all. Maybe there will be an earthquake in the middle of the night and the roads and airports will all be closed come morning."

I forced a smile. "Way to put a positive spin on things, dearest."

He gulped and shut his eyes. I doused the lights and blinked into the darkness. In ten minutes, I could hear him snoring. Me, I was wide-awake. Go figure.

In any case, the night came and went, minus any earthquakes. In the interim, I'd thought of a plan. Considering my lack of sleep and stress level, was it a good plan? Probably not. But it was, at the very least, a plan.

"Um, Ted," I heard, the sunshine through the curtains warming my face. "I think I've had a stroke."

"A stroke?" I asked, yawning as I did so. "I don't think you can talk all that well after you've had a stroke."

"But I can't move my arms or legs."

"Oh, that," I retorted, pushing myself up onto my elbows. "I tied you up in your sleep, Ron. So, in fact, you could move your arms and legs, if they weren't bound together." I pulled the blanket down to his feet and pointed. "See."

He stared down the length of him. He was in his boxers, his hands bound by some rope I'd found in the basement while he was conked out, his feet the same. Yippee for the Boy Scouts because I had several merit badges in rope tying to my credit. In other words, he wasn't going anywhere.

Save, that is, of course, to his wedding.

"You can't *make me* get married, Ted," he said, his eyes a tad wider now, fear quite evident on his otherwise handsome face.

"Wanna make a bet?" All in all, it was an apt reply, seeing as our wedding was in Las Vegas later that afternoon.

"Untie me, Ted."

I shook my head and hopped out of bed. "When we get to the hotel, Ron. In Vegas. In about four hours."

"I can't drive to Vegas, Ted," he whined. "I can't even get dressed like this."

I shrugged. "Your tux is in the trunk of our rental car. Your toiletries are in the trunk of our rental car. Your clothes for the weekend are in the trunk of our rental car." I walked to his side of the bed and stared down at him. "Keep complaining, Ron, and you'll be joining them there." I bent down and kissed him on the forehead. "Welcome to the happiest day of your life, hon."

Ten minutes later, I was dressed and Ron was, well, still in his boxers and still tied up, albeit in the front seat of the rental car and not the trunk. See, I wasn't a total monster. In fact, I was no monster at all. I was simply hoping (praying, crossing innumerable fingers and toes) that his second to ninth thoughts wouldn't manifest themselves between Los Angeles and Las Vegas.

"Is this how you want to remember our wedding day, Ted?" he asked, once we were on the freeway and a good way from home.

My shrug returned. "At least I'll *have* a wedding day, Ron."

He struggled with his bindings, the leather seat making scrunching noises beneath him. I listened as he yanked and pulled and tugged at the ropes. I turned my head to toss in a witty bon mot or two, at his expense, when I noticed that a) he was sweating and b) his boxers were tenting something fierce.

I pointed at his crotch. "What's that about?"

A flush of red worked its way across his cheeks. "Morning wood."

I stared back at the road. "That's for when you've just woken up. Try again." He didn't reply. I laughed as I realized what was happening. "You know what I think?"

Again he struggled. "That you're horrible for tying me up and dragging me to the altar?"

I shook my head. "Nope. That ain't it." I reached my hand across and gave his flimsily covered cock a squeeze. "I think you like this. I think you like being made to do what you can't make your mind up to do. I think you like the choice taken away from you. And..." I pulled his cock through the cottony slit. It popped free, leaking and thick. "And I think you like being tied up to boot." I quickly looked his way. "Maybe I should've gagged you, too."

The red on his face turned crimson, but, to be fair, the head of his cock did the same, a dribble of spunk bubbling up before leaking over the side. "You better not," he whined.

I laughed. Talk about your halfhearted comebacks. "Looks like my husband has a new kink in his chain."

"Not your husband," he yapped. "Not yet."

"Ah," I said, smacking his prick for good measure, and eliciting a moan from him for my troubles. "Then there's hope, after all." I reached my hand across the small divide and pinched his nipple. His body quivered and quaked, and, lo and behold, my own cock was suddenly straining from within my jeans. Which meant that both of our chains had newly apparent kinks in them.

"Live and learn," I murmured.

"Huh?" he panted.

I again turned his way. "Never mind." I gazed from his sweat-soaked brow to his throbbing prick, then to his bound wrists. "Gosh, you're beautiful, Ron."

He grunted. "When I'm immobilized, you mean."

I looked back down the road and continued to drive. "You say potato..."

A couple of hours later, we were finally in the desert. The highway had given way to a cracked, two-lane road, the traffic sparse. As for Ron, his cock would occasionally droop, but I remedied that each time with a smack across his belly or yank on his tender nipple. When I could no longer wait for the inevitable, I pulled off the road and found a dustier, even emptier path to travel along.

Deep within the Mojave, I finally pulled the car over, ours the only one in the bleak, barren lot, the brick bathroom to the side deeply sun-blanched. "Sit tight, hon," I said as I hopped out of the car.

"Funny," he barked, rigid cock swaying to and fro.

I ran around the car and opened his door. "Out."

He shook his head, pouting. "No."

I leaned in and grabbed both his nipples. He squirmed, moaned and promptly followed my lead. That is to say, he followed me as I yanked him out of the car by said pink appendages. Still, his feet were bound, so, though he could walk, it was in inches, and hopping would've taken too long. So I bent down and roughly flung him over my shoulder.

"Aren't we supposed to do this on our honeymoon, asshole?" he spat.

I spanked his ass. Twice. "That's for calling me an asshole on our wedding day."

"You hog-tied me on mine!" he retorted as we moved away from the car and behind the bathroom.

"Out of love," I replied as I set him down on a picnic bench that had seen better days. Though, to be fair, at least a spindly tree did provide a smidge of shade from the otherwise broiling sun. I then pushed him backward and relieved him of his boxers, and since he was hog-tied, that meant, *rrriiiip*, off they came, outward as opposed to the standard downward way.

"Hey!" he objected, though I heard it more as a *yay!* Let's blame it on the heat—of the moment.

I ran back to the car, shouting over my shoulder, "Now don't you move none."

He grumbled something. I turned, ran back, spanked his ass and again ran back to the car, returning with a bottle of water. Except, Ron was no longer on the bench when I returned, but instead was hopping miserably in my direction. Seeing as he'd disobeyed my direct command, and seeing as I'd wisely also brought the remainder of the rope, I herded him in reverse and began to tie him around the thankfully smooth yet spindly tree.

"What's your mom going to say when I tell her what you've done?" His face was red and his cock was so thick and steely that it could've cracked open a safe. Though what a waste of a perfectly good cock that would've been.

"What would she say?" I replied, standing back to observe

my work. The rope was now tied to his wrist bindings, wrapped thrice around the tree, and tied again to his feet restraints. Between two of the turns of rope, his cock jutted out, balls hanging over the cable. "She'd say, 'Told you those Boy Scout lessons would eventually come in handy.'"

He pulled and yanked at the tethering, though by then, it was only for show; my fiancé, as I've already said, wasn't going anywhere. Finally, he had no choice in the matter. And that, I assumed, was what was giving him that sensational-looking woody of his. As to my own rigid prick, it was being freed from its denim constraints a moment later, until I was just as hard and as naked as he was.

I closed the gap between us and squatted. My face moved into his crotch, the scent of sweat and musk and sex joyously wafting up my nostrils. I downed his cock in one fell swoop, tugging on his dangling balls as I did so. He moaned, loudly, legs buckling as I sucked, his cock pulsing down my throat.

I popped his cock out as I stroked my own with one hand and wiped a river of sweat off my face with the other. His beautiful prick glistened in the desert sun. I stroked it, fast and furious, his breath suddenly ragged, his knees fighting to stay locked. When he was close—years together had taught me to see and hear the warning signs—I yanked my hand free.

He exhaled sharply. "Fucker."

I chuckled. "That any way to talk to your soon-to-be husband?"

"You wish."

I nodded. "Yes, actually." Again I grabbed ahold of his throbbing tool. "Now, will you shut the fuck up, please?" In order to accomplish this next-to-impossible feat, I mashed my mouth into his, and his tongue, his only nonsecured body part, snaked and coiled with my own as we swapped some heavy spit and I jacked our pricks in sync.

His breathing quickly grew shallow, mine as well, as rivers of sweat cascaded down our bodies. Still, neither of these two things were on our minds when, for the last time as single men, we both spewed as one.

He exhaled sharply down my lungs, his body trembling as his cock erupted in an aromatic torrent of white-hot jizz, thick bands of which rocketed outward before landing in several splats on the arid ground below. My groan matched his moan as my own cock pulsed and shot, several streams of come flinging this way and that as I huffed and puffed, stars swimming before my sweat-stinging eyes.

A smile worked its way up his face as he fought to catch his breath. "Thank you," he managed to squeak out.

"For?" I replied.

He shrugged, as best he could. "For..." He stared down at his bindings and then over at me. "For everything." He laughed, his finely etched belly shaking as he did so, the rope shaking as well. "Gives a whole new meaning to the term."

My laugh matched his. "Tying the knot?"

"Exactly."

I wiped the sweat off his forehead, his cheek, his neck. "Are we still doing that?"

His smile widened, stretching across his damp, reddened face. "Of course, Ted," he replied. "Was there ever any doubt?"

I sighed as I began to untie him. "Never," I told him, fairly meaning it.

"Forever," he purred, watching my progress, or lack thereof. "Until death do us part."

I fell to the ground and stared up at him. "You, uh, you might have to wait for that in order to get untied from this tree, actually, Ron," I freely admitted. "Because they gave out merit badges for tying these suckers, not, sadly, untying them." My sigh repeated. "Do you think we can go for a round two and try to untie said knots after that?"

His grin remained, as did his stellar erection. "I do, Ted," he vowed. "I most certainly do."

BADDHA KONASANA

Corvidae

"Good job, Andrea, your posture is looking much better."

I grunt. I don't know what he's talking about. I can see my pose in the mirror. Everyone around me is hovering in a perfect chair pose, graceful as cranes. My pose looks more like a broken futon.

Tomas's hand brushes my lower back. In the mirror I see him nodding in approval. "You should be feeling this in the lumbar spine," he tells the class. "Feel the tension evenly on both sides, supporting your spine as you lengthen forward with your arms."

Of course there's tension in my spine; there's tension everywhere. There usually is whenever Tomas approaches my mat.

I started coming to yoga as part of a New Year's resolution, but after four months, I've realized that I'm not just coming here for my health. Listening to Tomas's smooth voice and watching his lean body flow through the movements like water soothe me in ways my poses never can. The struggling and the pain are almost worth it when he comes around to gently adjust and correct me, melting the tension in my muscles with his touch. Those brief touches are pretty much the only contact we have, besides my shy hello at the start of class and a breathless thank you and good-bye at the end.

Real breezy. It's a wonder he even knows my name...

"All right, gently come out of your *utkatasana,* pressing up with your heels. Keep your arms lifted, elongate both sides of the rib cage, then come down and prepare yourself for *savasana.*"

Thank god. Lying flat on my back. A pose I can actually accomplish. I flop down in relief and bury myself under an eye pillow. This is always my favorite part of class, lying in the warm dark, bathed by the even breathing of everyone around me, listening to Tomas pad around the room as he makes gentle adjustments where necessary. Usually I have no idea how uncomfortable I am until he moves me into a better position.

And I know it's a meditative pose, but you're supposed to let the thoughts drift without judgment, so how can anyone judge me if my mind usually goes to a very restless place, inviting Tomas along?

Today, though, I can't conjure my happy place. Days like today—when all I've done is struggle—I feel like an idiot, especially compared to all these lithe yoga kittens around me. The voice in the back of my mind tells me that I'm slowing everyone down, that I'm a hindrance to Tomas's lessons and the only reason he knows my name is because he looks for it on the sign-up roster in dread....

A series of soft chimes breaks the cycle. People around me start to stir. Wow, ten minutes already? Time sure flies when you're hating on yourself.

"Thank you everybody! *Namaste!*" Tomas's voice stirs the class back to life. "Remember, if you borrowed a mat, please wipe it down before returning. Megan's evening class today is cancelled, so no need to rush out of the studio."

I roll to a seat, bleary as a newborn. People around me are similarly disoriented, but gaining speed as they collect their blankets and props. I rub my eyes with the heel of my hand and lean over to do the same.

A familiar pair of feet stop in front of my mat. "Andrea," Tomas's voice drifts down. I gape up at him. From this angle he towers above me, a statue of *David* in Lycra and spandex. Even in the dim light of the studio, I can see his eyes smiling at me, emerald against his tan skin.

"Buh?" is all I can say.

"Andrea, do you have a couple minutes? I wanted to go over a couple suggestions for you, if that's all right."

I nod.

He smiles reassuringly. "Great, just hang tight for a sec. Richard had a quick question. I'll be right back."

He pads off. Only then do I realize that my jaw is still hanging open.

I sit on my mat, stewing in anxiety. What could he want? Am I doing something wrong? Is he going to make me switch to another class, better suited for amateurs? I pick up my yoga strap to wrap it, but start twisting and fiddling with it instead.

Tomas comes back as the last of the class passes through the curtain to the front lobby. I'm still focused on the strap and barely glance up as he drops down to a seat in front of me.

"Andrea," he says in the same calm yet commanding tone he uses to instruct the class. "I can tell that you're frustrated, but you have to understand, we call it yoga *practice* for a reason. It's never perfected. We're always learning and growing through our practice. And whether or not you believe it yet"—he leans forward and rests a consoling hand on my ankle—"you *are* making progress."

I shrug, still not looking up. This is already the longest conversation I've had with him, and I haven't even said anything yet. My breath is shallow from a combination of embarrassment and excitement.

"Some people describe yoga as 'a balance between effort and ease.' While you're engaging one part of your body, you should be relaxing and elongating others."

Ha. That's easy for him to say. It's easy to be relaxed and confident when you're already strong.

"You focus well," he continues, "but you're focused on the effort, with none of the ease. You trust my instructions but you also need to train your body to trust *itself*, trust the muscles that are doing the work, and relax the rest."

Yeah, well right now I don't even trust myself to not blush like a schoolgirl just by looking at him.

He watches me in silence for a few moments. I hunch over my mat, still not daring to look up. "I have an idea," he says suddenly, leaning over to grab my blanket. "Fold this up so it's at least four layers thick. Sit on the edge, with your feet below you in *baddha konasana*."

I put down the strap, arrange the blanket as he says, then hesitate.

"Bound cobbler pose," he prompts gently.

Ah, yes. Middle school PE butterfly stretch. I place the soles of my feet together in front of me and spread my knees wide. I grip and curl forward over my feet, not because you're supposed to, but because if I don't, my tight muscles will snap me out of it like an overwound rubber band.

He rolls up to his feet and paces around me. "Okay, take a second to check in. Do you feel how your muscles are fighting against themselves?"

"Mrrg," I respond.

There's a clank of metal hitting the floor. I risk a glance up. Tomas has my strap in his hands, spreading and untwisting it. The D-rings clink as they drag against the wood. We use straps in class all the time, so pulling it out is nothing strange.

What *is* strange is the look on Tomas's face. He's watching me intently, eyes drawing my gaze in and boring through it. His hands are moving purposefully, but slowly, letting the woven canvas pour through his fingers. His face is neutral, but I could swear I see the hint of a smirk tugging at the corners of his mouth.

"I want to try something," he says, kneeling next to me. "Something to help support you so your muscles can learn to relax. Is that all right?"

"Mrrg," I agree, nodding.

I watch as he folds the strap into a large loop, deftly manipulating the puzzle of the D-rings. I remain motionless as he leans over to settle the loop around me.

"Can I touch you?" he asks, his breath surprisingly close to my ear. I stifle a gasp and nod.

His hands brush against my back, sliding the strap down so that it rests against the crest of my hip. He loops the far edge of the circle under my clenched feet, then runs his hands along the strap to smooth out any folds, brushing against the curve of my waist and the insides of my thighs.

I shudder, but not from muscular strain.

"All right," he says finally, leaning close again. Whiffs of him drift over me, a subtle bouquet of sweat and incense. "Let me know if any of this starts to feel painful," he says. All I can do is nod, my beating heart choking my throat.

He starts cinching, the loop squeezing tighter around me as he pulls out the slack. His hands skate across the band, keeping it flush against my body, stroking my skin through the canvas.

My mind reels. It's way more contact than he gives anyone in class, but then he's never done anything like this in class before.

"How do you feel?" he asks.

I have no words to describe the sensations inside me, the thrill of being handled like this. Handled by him. Instead, I resort to my old standby: sarcasm. "Like a bundle of asparagus," I mutter, still bent awkwardly forward.

He chuckles. "I'm going to go a little farther. Again, let me know if you want me to stop."

I have no idea what he means, and honestly I'm doubtful whatever he's doing will work anyway, but right now I'm too dazed to protest. He pulls the loop tighter. The strap presses more insistently against my hips and thighs, gently pulling them toward my feet. It's wide enough that it doesn't pinch in painfully. All I feel is an unrelenting pressure—a pressure that is gradually increasing.

Tomas stops. "All right, Andrea," he says softly. "Let go of your feet and lean back."

I hesitate, muscles shivering with tension. My instincts say the minute I let go everything will splay open, like an *un*bundled bunch of asparagus. I glance up at Tomas. He smiles and places a hand lightly on my upper back, coaxing relaxation into the delicate skin between my shoulder blades.

"It's all right. Trust the strap, it's strong enough."

I exhale and let go.

My back cantilevers back to vertical. I spread my arms out, expecting to catch myself as I fall back on the mat.

But...I stay upright.

I look down, surprised. It's just a band, looped between my hips and feet, but somehow it feels like so much more. There's pressure on my back and under my feet, but the rest of me feels like it's floating. My bent knees are a good foot from the ground, but for once they aren't straining to remain that way.

"Very good, Andrea," Tomas's voice purrs from somewhere above me. "Now really relax into it."

I take a few deep breaths and close my eyes. My weight is settling farther into the strap, but it responds with equal, inexorable pressure. Shivers run along my spine as my nervous system tries to comprehend the sensation of being simultaneously restrained and exposed. My inner thighs are especially vulnerable, braced open by the grip of the strap. They tingle in protest but I breathe through it, just like Tomas has taught me.

When I open my eyes, my knees have drifted fractionally closer to the floor.

I look around the studio. Tomas is over by the shelf of props, digging through one of the baskets. The voices from the lobby have died out. I realize with a jolt that we may be the only people left in the entire place. I can't decide whether that's exciting or terrifying. It feels like both.

Tomas comes back with another strap, casually uncoiling it and dragging it behind him, smiling at me as he advances across the floor. My stomach flutters. I'm already in the pose; what could possibly be left for him to bind up?

"This is an interesting trick I learned years ago from...a teacher of mine." He winks at me. "This one is a little trickier to set up, but once you learn it you can do it on your own. Do you want to try?"

I nod mutely. He drops to his knees on the back of my mat, thighs and abdomen hovering just inches behind me.

"Lift up your hair," he says in his class voice, a voice I've been conditioned for four months to obey unquestioningly. I comply, gathering it up and holding it with both hands.

"Good," he says. "Keep your arms lifted like that." He brushes his fingers across the back of my neck, then drapes the midpoint of the strap across it, letting the loose ends fall down my front on either side. His breath tickles my skin as he leans over my shoulder, adjusting and untwisting the strap. I remain still, not even twitching an elbow until he tells me to.

He flattens the band and pulls both ends back under my arms, wrapping them around my shoulders and armpits like backpack straps. "You may drop your arms," he murmurs, face inches from my ear. "If you can, fold them behind you, clasping opposite elbows."

Once again I instinctively obey, pressing my forearms against my low back. This position thrusts my chest slightly forward, but also lifts it. Tomas pulls the ends of the strap tight under my arms, which spreads and lifts my chest farther.

I squirm, feeling uncomfortably exposed yet again.

His arms press into me as he crosses the strap behind my back, feeding the ends under my arms and back to my front. I can't see him, so each unexpected touch sends a spark of electric surprise through me. I suppress my shudders, concentrating instead on the invigorating sensation spreading in my chest and hips.

He crawls around to my other side and picks the strap back up again, face calm and focused—the same expression he gets when he's demonstrating a particularly difficult pose. His movements are lithe and efficient, also like his poses in class. He loops the strap through the rings and cinches it across my ribs, just under my breasts.

Just like with the first strap, once it's settled he pulls it tighter. My body jerks with the motions, but I relax into it. Each contraction pulls my shoulders farther back and my chest forward, my arms and neck muscles protesting the new position. I ache to move and stretch them out, but I keep my arms clasped as instructed.

He leans back on his heels, observing me with a pleased grin.

"Right. Now, relax, breathe deep, but don't arch your back. Let the pressure of the straps guide you into a strong, stacked posture." He lifts himself to his feet in one motion, then steps back.

He told me to breathe deeply, but I can barely breathe at all. He's pacing, critically evaluating me as if we're in an art gallery instead of a yoga studio and I'm some curious sculpture. I quiver, instinctively wanting to fold in on myself, to shelter my body like I shelter my thoughts. Instead, I am bared before him.

I finally take a breath, feeling it rush into new areas of my lungs, stretching underused back muscles. My legs, too, have relaxed farther, opening and exposing my pelvis. The angle of my shoulders straightens my neck and lifts my head higher.

I sit and breathe, a tingle settling across my mind, similar to the tingles dancing along my muscles. I am anchored by the straps and Tomas's instructions, prevented from moving the way my body instinctively wants to move. But at the same time, it feels like a part of me is drawing upon that external restraint, and my secret places—so callously exposed—are absorbing the energy of his gaze and growing stronger from it.

As that energy fills me, warms me, I feel drawn toward him in return.

I sit for ages, mind reeling with conflicting feelings, Tomas watching intently the entire time. Finally he smiles, almost sadly. "Very good, Andrea, that's probably enough for now." He kneels down, leaning close to grab the strap. "Your pectoral muscles are probably tight so I don't want to—"

I kiss him.

It's not much of a kiss—all I can reach is the corner of his mouth, and honestly I am as surprised by it as he is—but the moment my lips touch his skin the energy pulsing between us swells and washes over me like fire.

He hesitates, pulling away gently, his face unreadable. The fire in my core turns to ice.

Craaaaaap, what the hell did I do, I look like an idiot and I'm all tied up so I can't even run…

He kisses me back, deeply, hungrily, his hands gripping my shoulders and sliding along my arms, which are still clasped behind my back. The fire in me stokes again, so high I barely comprehend what's happening. He pulls me toward him. His fingers digging into my skin convince me that this is actually real, not another *savasana* fantasy. Joy rushes through me, catapulting my excitement higher. I strain against the strap, trying to press closer.

His kisses descend. "God, Andrea," he growls against my neck, "you are so beautiful right now." His voice has become something new, deeper and more focused than even his class voice. A brief thrill of fear shoots through me. Who is this man, really? For the last four months, all I've seen is the calm, patient yoga teacher, but now…

I wobble as he pulls me toward him, hands sliding down the curve of my back to cup the soft swell of my ass in my shorts. I groan and lean closer, four months' worth of fantasies rushing into my head at once. I want those hands covering every inch of me, possessing all of the places they merely teased at before. I want his heat and his breath to overwhelm mine, drawing me out of my cautious self and to new heights.

Most importantly, I want him deep in the core he has so carefully coaxed open.

The sensation overload stuns my voice to silence. I whimper and thrust, trying to bring my aching need closer, a need that has been building since the first time I met him.

"You want more?" he chuckles, tracing fingers along the inside of my thigh and the edge of my shorts.

"Yes," I manage to gasp out.

He glances toward the lobby. My eyes follow. The curtain is closed, hiding us from the front windows, and the front door is probably locked, but with the number of teachers that work at the studio, any one of them could let themselves in at any moment. My stomach flips at the thought.

But my excitement also increases.

"All right," he murmurs, fingers brushing against my crotch. "It *is* fitting to end a practice with the proper relaxation, after all." He crawls behind me, slithering his hands down my front, pulling me firmly against his chest. I moan, rolling my head back, exposing my neck for him to devour more. One hand grips the strap under my breast, securing me against him. The other slides down my abdomen and works its way into my shorts.

This time there is no teasing, no tantalizing touches. His fingers—rough, strong—grip me possessively, cupping my mound and working their way under my panties. I gasp at the sudden intrusion, straining against the straps to open myself to it more. Two of his fingers slide through my folds, spreading and searching. The moment they find their destination they plunge inside.

I gasp again, louder, and arch my back, but his grip on the strap keeps me close. "Try and keep your spine stacked," he whispers in my ear, laughter in his voice. I nod, moaning as he works his way in deeper. His fingers flex and flutter, sending waves of electricity through me. I open up farther, feeling my juices soaking through my overpriced shorts. He dives in farther, sliding his thumb up to massage from outside as well. I squirm against the protective grip of his arms and the straps, simultaneously trying to escape the sensations and absorb more.

"Relax," he growls, kissing my ear. "Let me do the effort, you focus on the ease."

I nod, jaw agape. “Harder,” I squeak out breathlessly. He complies, pulling me closer against him. The tension in my body increases, every breath drawing it higher, pressing against the straps until I feel I’ll burst.

“Come for me, Andrea,” he whispers in his instructor’s voice, breath heavy in my ear.

I immediately obey.

The strain wound up inside me snaps. I cry out, my voice echoing off the clean empty walls of the studio. His arms clench as I shudder, binding me tighter than the straps. Supported like this, I surrender fully to the hot jolts of pleasure rising through me, letting myself quiver, trusting in the strength of his arms and the bands to hold me in place.

Slowly my passion fades, replaced by a warm fog. My body relaxes, but the external braces keep me in position. I lean my head back against his chest. He kisses my neck again.

Wordlessly, he starts to un-cinch the straps. My body sags as their support fades, but I keep my arms and legs folded until the bands are fully removed. Once they are, I stretch out slowly, muscles singing in pleasure and relief.

Tomas climbs to his feet and reaches out to lift me up as well. He pulls me against him for a kiss again, tenderly this time.

“I hope that was…illustrative,” he murmurs.

I nod, my brain still too wispy to form complete words.

He chuckles and kisses my hands. “But really, strapping you up wasn’t just for my benefit. Here, look…” He stands back and points to my reflection in the mirror.

Even though the straps are gone, my shoulders are still rolled slightly back, spreading my chest open and noticeably lifting my head. My legs, too, are standing broad and even. It’s as if the ghosts of the straps are still wrapped around me, creating a posture of strength, and confidence.

"I want you to keep these feelings—this strength, this play between effort and ease—in mind during your next class," he says. "You always have this inside you, all you need is to practice."

I turn back to him. His face is calm, but his eyes glitter mischievously. "Do you have any questions?" he asks.

"Yes, actually," I mutter, smiling shyly. "Do you do private lessons?"

QUEEN FOR A NIGHT

Robert Black

I don't believe it occurred to Sara that her seat seemed a lot like a throne.

I am sure she was unaware that regal tribute was waiting at her feet. But I know she knows how much I like to study the stars—and how proud I am of giving gifts the recipient never forgets.

We were all but alone at my cabin in the pines. It was her birthday, August 12, the night of peak activity for the Perseids. I'd told her years ago that there was magic in her arrival, that she was born under a shower of lucky stars in flight.

At times she has found it difficult to believe in her sidereal good fortune. Tonight she was in for a surprise that could not fail to elevate Sara's assessment of herself.

As we relaxed beneath a silky new moon, the heavens were sporadically vivid with flares of white in the deep blue stillness before dawn. Head back, eyes bugging, Sara giggled as a meteor cut a long bright scratch through the ink of the clear northern sky. We sat on the deck together in matching outdoor chairs—outsized and overpriced, elegantly molded of hard plastic, with tapered slats like stylized sun rays defining each fan back.

Her feet rested on her unopened present, a box six feet long, three feet high and three wide. I had covered it in purple cloth, tucking the excess fabric carefully beneath, and topped it with a spray of evening primrose I'd arranged to look like a bow.

Ice hissed as it melted in the near-empty pitcher of mojitos on top of the box. My barefoot best friend extended a big toe to toy with one of the lemony petals in the bouquet.

"They open in the evening and close in the morning," she said, still looking up.

"So will you," I said, nudging the box with my heel.

"What are you talking about?" Sara was starting to slur; *Perfect,* I thought, rising to my feet.

"How long has it been since you've had your kinks worked out?" I asked, my back to the rail just behind her.

"What's with the riddles?" she replied.

In lieu of a response I dug my thumbs into the ropes of muscle at her lower neck and started to tug at her shoulders. The green tumbler slid out of her limp left hand and fell a few inches to land upright on mahogany.

Sara purred down low in her chest, leaned back and stretched her legs up and out in full. "Mmm...but don't hover over me, hon. I don't want to miss the fireworks."

"There's no danger of that." I nudged her pits and she lifted her arms so I could work the tension down and out of her fingers. I used to practice on Sara when I studied for a long minute to become a massage therapist; she picked up the drill shortly before I dropped the inclination.

"Since when have you been well taken care of?" Another trick question; I knew she had been chastely single since her son of a bitch of a boyfriend cut her loose with a semiliterate text message almost three months ago.

"A night like this is more than I could hope for," she said. "And besides, there are limits on the things...friends can do for one another."

"Not as many as you might think," I said, taking my hands away. "How come you haven't been asking about your gift?"

"I figured you'd show me when you were ready." Sometimes her passivity gets under my skin a little. Tonight it would play directly into my perverse little hands.

"Almost," I said, leaning back and looking up. "Do you remember the shooting star we saw a moment ago?"

"Mmm," she said again, eyes closed in what I assumed was recollection. "What about it?"

"That flare cut through the constellation of Cassiopeia. Turn around in your chair and look up.

"It's named after a vain queen, who boasted about her unrivaled beauty."

"Sounds like someone I know," Sara said, ass out, eyes skyward.

"You should try arrogance once in a while," I said. "It works wonders for me.

"Will you do me a favor, sweetie?" My friend knew well the tone I use when I tiptoe toward plain speaking.

"What?" she asked, head back, eyes wider, lids heavy with liquor and distilled ambience. Her easy sincerity always charms and endears me. Under my roof it was all conveyed in code. With Sara I could be straight and plain.

"Please don't jump away when we open your present...just go with me on this one."

"What are you getting at?"

"Look up, hon. Those five stars define Cassiopeia." I sucked down half my drink in one gulp. "It's shaped like a *W.* As in woman. And wanton. And why not."

I paused, then I pleaded. "Do you promise not to jump? To accept your present in the spirit in which it is given?"

"Jesus Christ, yes," she said. "When the fuck am I going to get it?"

"Now," I said, throwing my tumbler over the rail. "Turn around, your majesty. Remember your promise. And enjoy."

I lifted the cloth before Sara to reveal the front door of a cage. A puppy cage, as it's known in the trade: All-steel construction, fully welded and powder-coated, with round three-quarter inch bars for a smooth clean look.

Behind the bars cowered the prize in the Cracker Jacks: a smooth, clean-looking young man, fully muscled and oil coated, with steel wrist shackles hooked to matching lengths of chain running up to his sturdy bondage collar.

The chains were a custom order, long enough so my darling pet could lift his head—which he knew not to do when I opened the door and led him out by the leash affixed to his choker.

At which point Sara broke her promise, scrabbling like an upturned beetle to right herself, regain her poise and flee.

"Hold it, sweetie," I said, my back to the cat that had not yet emerged from his bag.

"You're out of your fucking skull," Sara said, seated now and trying to rise. I caught her partway with a hand on each shoulder.

"You promised not to jump."

"This is wrong," Sara said, "on so many levels. I don't know where to start."

"*He knows* where."

"Stop clowning, Jess. This has to stop. *Now.*"

"Nothing has started, hon. Please sit down. And listen to me."

I knelt on the deck at her feet with my ass close enough to his face to feel his breath thereupon. He knew better than to move a muscle.

I caught Sara's furtive glance at my captive and endeavored to tease out the devil in her.

"Tell me what you think is wrong."

She laughed and shook her head. I bent my back to chase her gaze, to catch it and hold it gently.

"You've got to be kidding me," she said.

"I've seldom been this serious. *Please* tell me what you think is wrong."

"Okay, damn it," Sara said. "You can't keep people in cages, like you're running some kind of perverted petting zoo."

"Yes I can, sweetie," I said. "We don't have to feed the animal, but I can keep him, for as long as he wants to be kept."

She shook her head slowly, looked down, got a rich eyeful before she looked away. And looked back, then said, eyes skyward, "Then where the fuck do you get off keeping this poor *bastard* in handcuffs?"

I resisted the temptation to suggest that she could easily imagine where I got off and on in this roundelay. "I must confess that sometimes he gets a little too free with his hands," I said. "And also, he appreciates the challenge of tending to his *dutie*s without them."

Sara's eyes were now stone-sober wide, pupils big and dark in a manner reflecting something beyond indignation. I did not have to look to know that my pet remained kneeling, his eyes to the wood.

"And what on earth is the matter with *him*, that he wants to be kept this way?"

"Please look at me, sweetie. And listen for a long minute." She stared. I drew a deep breath. "This is going to sound medium cold, I suppose, but it's the god's truth as I've learned it. I don't inquire about what's in his heart. Just asking the question would suggest that I think something is *wrong* with him. And with *me*. I don't see it that way. It *thrills me* to know I can capture his spirit and sport with his flesh as I please. *As you please.* What's in his heart is none of my business."

Gone stiff, Sara leaned back in her chair. I flashed on the vintage Maxell cassette ad, with the impassive seated man blown theatrically backward by powerhouse high fidelity.

I nudged the mojito glass toward her limp fingers and soldiered on, grasping for poise.

"Lean in, hon. He doesn't need to hear this."

She did. And I was sure he did too.

"This may strike you as strange, but they line up like jets at Newark International for the *privilege* of being where he is."

Sara met my eyes squarely for the first time in the last three minutes. "Get the fuck out of here," she said.

"Isn't that true, my pet?"

"Yes," he said, then was done talking.

For the first time, Sara sized him up in the manner I'd been hoping to see: like a lobster tail in a chafing dish at a sumptuous Lucullan banquet. He was a former competition swimmer, with the wide shoulders, broad chest and ropy muscles common to his appetizing breed. I turned to face him, reached in and pulled off the gold sash that girdled his loins. His large meaty cock bobbed in earnest, perpendicular to his flat belly, a love soldier standing proudly at attention.

I tugged at his leash. He crawled to the edge of Sara's chair. She tensed but did not retreat. "Isn't he lovely, dear?"

"Yes," Sara said with a quiver. Or whimper.

Another pull and he eased in closer, before Sara could close her legs.

"Haven't you ever given pleasure to a man and received none of your own in return?"

She threw her head back, bellowed, "Stop it!" and saw the mother of all celestial fireworks slash a brilliant trail through Andromeda. Bold and bright, the streak of light pulsed for five exquisite seconds through the grand constellation named for Cassiopeia's daughter, also known in reverberant legend as the Chained Lady.

"Oh my god," Sara said. On cue, the chained man buried his head beneath her skirt and nuzzled her mound with his nose. He tugged her panties to one side with a deft motion of his lips and buried his long tongue inside her. He licked and kissed and serviced her attentively as Sara sank back in her chair.

Still on all fours, he looked up at Sara, gray eyes going from shy to sly in the slightest narrowing of his eyelids. Then he yanked at the bonds on his wrists, his chains clinking in the heavy silence.

Sara looked down at him and started to smile. She eased her legs apart and he slid his tongue back into her pussy—drawing it upward, pressing it flat, then easing out to make wet warm contact with the hood of her swollen sweet spot.

She petted his head, leaned back and cooed. He took her clit between his lips and tugged at it lightly while drawing a breath. Her calves on his back, she slumped in her chair to give him better access. He sighed in joy, which made Sara giggle. He answered with sensuous swirls of his tongue—dirty, deliberate, around and around.

"Oh my god," Sara said again. "Oh fucking god, you win." He lapped at her now, all languor and patience, from the cleft of her bottom to the crown of her bliss. She began rocking her hips in lewd rhythm, slow and deliberate, fucking his face.

"What's your name, sweetie?" she whispered.

"Happy birthday," I said and went inside.

* * *

The cage was not as heavy as it looked. Its six sides detached easily and were stored discreetly.

The same could be said of its praiseworthy inhabitant, who by arrangement had put away the hardware and made himself scarce before sunrise. I had discreetly taped to his trim lovely flesh the key to free himself from his bonds. I leave you to imagine where.

At just after eleven, I was gratified to see Sara in bent spent angelic repose on the sofa to the left of the sunroom door. Her ash-blonde hair was a riot of clump and tangle; she had never changed out of her sundress. I spread a second blanket over my homegirl and read a little while the coffee brewed.

According to legend, Cassiopeia was arrogant and vain.

She bragged that both she and her daughter were more lovely than all the Nereids, the nymph-daughters of the sea god Nereus. This incurred the wrath of Poseidon, ruling god of the sea.

He placed her in the heavens tied to a chair so that, as she circles the celestial pole in her throne, she is upside down half the time. The constellation resembles the chair that originally represented an instrument of torture.

"Each to her own myths," I said to myself as Sara began to stir on the couch.

BOUND TO LIE

Nichelle Gregory

"Mr. Leland and Mr. Falconi will be with you shortly, Ms. Tesser."

Lexie glanced up from her leather portfolio and smiled at Gloria. "Thank you."

The receptionist peered at her over her glasses. "Can I get you anything to drink? Coffee, water?"

Lexie lifted her hand. "Oh, no. Thank you."

Gloria nodded before directing her attention to her computer. Lexie looked at her watch as her stomach growled. She never ate before completing a mission. An empty belly kept her focused and she looked forward to enjoying a meal afterward. Lexie was glad all she needed was information this time. Later, she would celebrate her impeccable record with the company and indulge with lobster bisque and a large slice of double-chocolate cake. She planned to savor that dessert in less than an hour.

The phone on Gloria's desk rang and Lexie listened to her quick replies. She knew the other woman had been given her final directives before she could head home and that she'd been made aware of Mr. Leland's late arrival. In less than twenty minutes Gloria would leave and she would be alone with Mr. Dane Falconi. Lexie drew a pen from her bag.

Dane Falconi thought he was about to review possible concepts for a nightclub that would no doubt rival New York's finest. He had no idea the havoc she was about to wreak once the two of them were left to take care of business. Lexie toyed with the slim gold ballpoint while pretending to study the intricate designs before her as Gloria hung up the phone.

"Ms. Tesser?"

Lexie lifted her head. "Yes?"

"Mr. Leland has been delayed in his commute from the airport, but Mr. Falconi can see you now." Gloria got up and rounded her desk. "Please come with me."

"Of course." Lexie closed her portfolio, slipped it into her bag and stood, pleased to be right on schedule.

She followed Gloria around the corner, noting the exit at the end of the hallway as they passed panels of glass giving views into empty office spaces. Lexie didn't bother eyeing her reflection, confident her appearance was every bit as flawless as the work she was about to present. She'd chosen a black high-waist pencil skirt and a heather-gray blouse with every intention of using her muted feminine wiles to distract Dane. She'd read his file several times. Dane enjoyed women like his coffee, rich and full-bodied.

"Here we are." Gloria knocked once on the door, then twisted the silver knob and opened it.

"Thank you." Lexie stepped past her into the midsized, well-designed conference room, eager to finish what she'd come to do.

"Ms. Tesser, welcome." Dane Falconi picked up his coffee

cup as he got up from the head of a beautiful dark wood table. He moved toward her, elegant and handsome as hell in a dark suit that matched his thick hair. "I apologize for my partner not being able to join us."

Lexie shook his offered hand. He seemed even taller than she knew him to be as his warm fingers grasped hers. "I understand. It's a pleasure meeting you, Mr. Falconi."

"Likewise." Dane turned his attention to his secretary. "Gloria, can you refresh my cup before you go?"

Dane had coffee at the end of each day. Lexie always appreciated the marks that were consistent. Made her work a hell of a lot easier. She loathed unexpected surprises, messy scenarios and any unaccounted variable that prolonged her from finishing a job.

"Of course." Gloria took Dane's cup and exited the room.

"Mr. Falconi, I'm excited to show you these concepts this evening." Lexie gripped the pen tighter in her left hand as she followed him along the opposite side of the polished rectangle table, ensuring her seat would be to his right.

"Please, call me Dane." He waited for her to sit down before doing the same. "Your firm comes so highly recommended. I know taking on a project already in progress isn't something your company normally does."

Lexie smiled, amused by Dane's ironic choice of words. She took her portfolio out of her bag she'd placed on the chair beside her. "It's our pleasure to help you and Mr. Leland build the kind of hot spot you're both known for."

Her *company* could pull off anything at the last minute; waking an architect in the middle of the night to whip up a few designs and forging her credentials was nothing.

"Let's see what you've brought." Dane scooted his chair closer to hers.

Lexie directed his attention to the first design. "Here, you'll see we've integrated—"

A soft knock on the door drew both their attention to Gloria coming in with two mugs on a tray and a file folder under her arm. "Pardon the interruption. This fax just came in for you."

Lexie would have to buy Gerard another bottle of his favorite vodka for his uncanny ability to always know the precise moment to engage her target.

Gloria placed the tray within reach, handed Dane his coffee and the folder, then smiled at Lexie. "There's hot water in the carafe along with a selection of teas and hot chocolate in case you change your mind about having something to drink."

Lexie gave the secretary a genuine smile. "How thoughtful."

A certain premium blend of cocoa was one of her guilty little pleasures.

"Thank you, Gloria." Dane opened the folder as Lexie glanced at the empty mug in front of her, half tempted to make the warm drink. She needed no distractions with her window of opportunity coming up in less than seven seconds.

Lexie watched Dane read the fax as the silver-haired clerk gave a faint nod of her head. "Do you need anything else before I go, Mr. Falconi?"

Dane shifted his attention from the paper in his hand to look at his executive assistant as Lexie prepared to make her move.

"That's all. Good night, Gloria."

Lexie kept her eyes on them both while she edged her hand imperceptibly closer to Dane's cup. She poised her pen above the rim and successfully depressed the whisper-quiet button on top that released the hidden liquid inside.

Success!

Lexie said good night to Gloria as she left. She heard the door click shut as Dane drank his coffee. One sip was all it usually took. She'd have him spilling his guts in no time. Lexie's gaze slid over Dane's face. He was an attractive man, clearly used to the world bending to his will. She would take pleasure in making him yield to hers in just a few minutes.

"Now, where were we?" Dane tapped his finger on her schematic. "I think you were just about to tell me how you integrated both metal and wood on the entrance of the building?"

"Yes. Mr. Leland expressed an interest in using eco-friendly materials over the phone. I also propose installing solar-powered skylights."

Dane put his cup down and nodded. "I love that idea."

"I thought you would." Lexie observed him squeeze the bridge of his nose, knowing he'd never hear the rest. "I've got several more concepts I think you'll like too."

"Are you sure you won't have a cup of cocoa?" He lifted the silver tin from under a napkin on the tray and Lexie recognized it as her favorite. "This is a really good brand. Very smooth."

Lexie smiled. "I think I just might."

Why not? Dane was already feeling the effects of the drug. Her long day was almost over. She deserved a few sips of pleasure. Lexie took the tin and the spoon Dane offered. She carefully added the powder and stirred as he poured water into her mug. The sweet fragrance wafted upward and Lexie couldn't resist tasting the cocoa.

"Delicious, isn't it?"

Lexie nodded. "Heavenly. Just what I needed."

"I thought another cup of coffee was just..." Dane frowned. "Just what I..." He blinked and looked at her. "What were we talking about?"

Lexie sat her drink down with a barely repressed grin.

He was ready and so was she.

"Do you remember my name, Mr. Falconi?"

Dane slowly blinked as he loosened his tie. "D-Dane. Please call me, Dane."

Lexie got up out of her seat. "Very well." She walked over to the door, locked it, then proceeded to close all the blinds. She turned to face Dane again, delighted to see he hadn't moved an inch. He continued to stare off into space as she moved back to her bag. She took out a mini-tape recorder and two plastic ties. "Dane, I need to ask you a few questions."

"What's going on?" He asked the question slowly, as if it were a struggle to say three words.

Lexie was impressed he'd spoken without slightly slurred speech. Sometimes that made understanding the intel she extracted difficult...but never impossible.

"What's going on right now is an exchange of information from you to me."

Dane leaned back in his chair. "Information? I don't...understand."

The initial effect of the drug she'd administered was disorientation, which was helpful for restraining her marks—for their safety and hers. Lexie preferred clean jobs with no blood, little sweat and no tears.

The latter usually occurred whenever she questioned a female, which was why Lexie favored interrogating members of the opposite sex. She never got tired of watching the medically induced cobwebs cleared away after she'd secured a man. Astonishment shifted to indignation, then outrage and finally, usually, they made the decision to give her what she wanted. Those were the easy guys. The harder ones, the ones that refused to cooperate...well, they got a visit from an operative within another branch of her company. They didn't mind getting dirty.

Lexie moved behind Dane. She rested her hands on the back of his chair, then leaned forward to whisper in his ear. "You don't need to understand. Now, tell me everything you know about Mr. Swan."

"Swan? He runs one of our nightclubs."

"I'm aware of that." Lexie ran a finger across the fabric of Dane's tailored suit. She turned him in the chair to face her. "Did you know he installed a state-of-the-art safe in his office?"

"Yes." Dane glowered. "What the hell is going on here? W-what did you give me?"

Lexie placed a hand on his shoulder when he attempted to get up. "Dane, I need you to focus." She caressed the top of his hand, which was resting on the metal arm of his seat. "Tell me what I need to know. There are files kept in that safe that are crucial to national security."

Hazel eyes locked with hers, captivating and arresting. Damn.

He had to be one of the sexiest marks she'd ever had the pleasure of tying down.

Pushing the errant thought from her mind, Lexie blinked, moved and within the breadth of a second secured Dane's wrist to the chair with her plastic tie.

"What do you think you are doing?" His voice had deepened with anger.

Lexie sighed. Sexy or not, she wanted this job done twenty minutes ago. She placed her palm on top of his other wrist. "Dane, I'll ask the questions. Okay, sweetie?"

"I don't think so." He grabbed her arm with his free hand and Lexie gasped.

Instinctually, she lifted her hand with every intention of striking his windpipe but Dane moved faster, placing his long fingers around her neck. Lexie's eyes widened as he squeezed, cutting off her air supply with cold-blooded efficiency. She only had a few precious seconds to react before she wouldn't be able to move at all. Dane smiled at her, his gaze steady, deadly as he tightened his grip around her esophagus.

Lexie grabbed at his hand with both of hers, desperation setting in as the need for oxygen switched her into survival mode. She clawed at him, but she knew just like Dane did that her efforts were futile as her vision began to blur. Shocked, Lexie stared up into the sepia depths of Dane's eyes as her fingers fell from his hand at her neck and she gave in to the blackness consuming her.

Dane checked the blood flow to Lexie's hands and ankles a final time before standing to admire his handiwork. She was secure on top of the conference table, her beauty on display. He didn't want to take his eyes off of her. Her outfit was perfect, professional and modest and fucking distracting.

The picture in Lexie's file didn't do her or her curves any damn justice. He'd released her hair from the clip holding the tresses back and now the curly ebony strands framed her face, in lush contrast to her caramel skin.

Dane moved from between her legs to her side. "Lexie, wake up."

Lexie remained still, except for the even rise and fall of her chest. Dane assessed the reddened marks around her throat as he took her pulse. It truly was a shame to mar such lovely skin, but she'd left him no choice. He trailed a finger down her cheek while studying the increase of eye moment beneath Lexie's eyelids. She was coming around.

"Lexie..."

One would never think she was capable of doing what Dane knew she could do. He smiled as Lexie slowly opened her eyes and looked at him. "Welcome back."

A flicker of emotion glimmered in the dark brown eyes

holding his and it only took Dane a nanosecond to recognize it wasn't fear, but anger that he found sexy as hell.

Dane watched Lexie lift her head and take stock of her current situation. She attempted to wrench her bound hands above her head, then more gingerly tested the nylon rope binding her ankles to the legs of the fine wood table.

"What do you want?" Her voice was steadier than the last male subject he'd unpleasantly surprised.

"Information."

Lexie laughed, and the husky sound made Dane's cock twitch. He admired her ability to remain calm after realizing there was no escape from whatever was about to happen next. She'd been trained for any scenario, but Dane had seen many with similar backgrounds fold minutes after accepting they were no longer in control.

Lexie glanced at his mug. "You faked me out."

"No, I drank the drug. I've just built up a tolerance for the amount you gave me."

"Who are you?"

Dane pressed his finger against Lexie's lips. "I'll ask the questions. Okay, sweetie?" He smirked when she glared at him.

"You'll get nothing out of me." Lexie turned her head away from him. "I'll never say a word."

"You aren't the first person to say that. Lexie, look at me." Dane took hold of her chin when she didn't respond and brought her face back to his. "We can do this the hard way or my way. I really would prefer not to hurt you, but you and I both know how this job has to be done. So tell me, what's it going to be?"

Dane shook his head as Lexie held his gaze and remained silent without flinching. Impressive.

She was as brave as she was gorgeous. The only indication he'd gotten to her was the increased flutter of her carotid pulse.

"Okay, Lexie, I'm going to give you a chance to talk despite your resolution against it." He moved his hands up to her blouse. Her eyes widened as he unfastened the little gray buttons and exposed her lacy black bra. Dane cupped her breasts and Lexie yanked once on the ropes restraining her hands. "What was your mission, Lexie?"

"Fuck you."

The two words were as cold and sharp as shards of ice. Dane chuckled as he pushed down the cups of her bra and exposed her dark chocolate nipples. He circled Lexie's areolas with his fingers, watched her suck in a breath as her flesh puckered beneath his touch. Dane flicked the hardening tips, then pinched them, making Lexie gasp. "What was your mission, Lexie?" He increased the pressure on her nipples as he pulled on them.

Dane could see Lexie's jaw tighten. She was uncomfortable, but he wasn't causing her any real pain, not the kind of pain he knew she anticipated, no matter how calm she managed to appear.

"Go to hell."

Dane released his hold on her and Lexie groaned. He put one hand on the table and leaned in close. "You first." Dane moved his head down, taking Lexie's breast into his mouth. She shrieked when he toyed with her nipple between his teeth. He nipped it and she again pulled against the binds holding her in place. Dane teased her other breast with his fingers while suckling, licking and kissing the one beneath his lips. He lifted his head when Lexie's frightened gasps turned into almost inaudible whimpers of pleasure. "What was your mission, Lexie?"

"I could tell you but then I'd have to kill you." Lexie shuddered as Dane chuckled.

She really was something else.

He rubbed his palm over both of her swollen nipples, then

moved toward the head of the table to stand between her legs. "I admire your fortitude." Dane glanced at his watch. "I'm afraid we need to hurry things along here." He reached into his suit jacket, pulled out his trusted Swiss Army knife and showed it to Lexie. "You know how this works. Make things easier on yourself. Tell me what I want to know."

Lexie snorted. "I *do* know how this works. We both know the game. We're both players. You can *try* to break me." She smiled at him. "Maybe I'll say something useful, maybe not, but we both know I'm bound to lie."

"Possibly." Dane pushed his knife between the fabric of her skirt and her thigh. He turned the blade outward and cut a deep slit, revealing more of her leg. "But you're underestimating just how good I am at my job."

"Likewise." Lexie briefly closed her eyes as he cut the other side of her skirt. "Nothing I say or don't say will change what you plan to do to me."

"You know?" Dane pushed her hem up and bared her panties. "That's where you're wrong." He traced an embroidered flower on the front panel of her lingerie and Lexie tensed. "These are pretty. Pretty and wet. Interesting."

That got a reaction. Dane felt a tremor flow through Lexie's body as she averted her face from him. He slipped his blade beneath the minuscule scrap of lace on each side of her hip, sliced and then tugged, revealing her shaved pussy as he pulled the damp panties free.

Dane squeezed her wet lips, dipped his finger between them and caressed her clit. Lexie's sharp intake of breath made his cock hard. He removed his hand, came to her side again, brought her ruined panties up to her face and pressed them against her nose. "Do you like being taken roughly, Lexie?" Dane didn't expect a response and he didn't get one, except for the goose bumps rising beneath his questing fingers on her inner thigh. "Do you look forward to those rare moments when you take a lover, relinquish control and let him fuck you? Look at me."

When she turned her head to meet his gaze, the brief glimpse of pain Dane saw in her eyes almost made him feel guilty. "You're a bastard." She trembled when he dropped the panties by her cheek and moved back between her bound legs.

That he was.

A bastard with a job to finish.

Lexie gritted her teeth as Dane spread her thighs wider, opening her to his view. She fought to remain still as he went back to playing in her betraying wetness, lubricating his fingers in her juices. Trying to move was pointless. Lexie had never felt so helpless. She clearly was in the last moments of her life and she couldn't accept it, couldn't fathom this was truly happening to her.

Dane swirled his finger over her clit, stirring up a helpless hunger. The reality was this *was* happening and she *was* enjoying it.

Lexie shifted her face from Dane's, tears burning her eyes. She wasn't going to cry; no way would she let him see her come undone.

Lexie yelped when Dane swatted her inner thigh.

"Keep your eyes on me."

Exhaling, she turned her head and met his gaze over her still embarrassingly hard nipples as he pushed his two middle fingers into her. The shock of him filling her, and facing how wet she truly was, drew another gasp from Lexie. She watched him place his other hand on top of her pussy. Lexie parted her lips to speak, then closed them. What could she say to stall him?

All thoughts fled her mind when he began rigorously finger-fucking her. The angle of his fingers coupled with the pressure of his hand on top of her pelvic bone was so intense, it consumed her senses. Lexie involuntarily closed her eyes as she moaned, arching her back off the table. Her chest heaved as she struggled not to whimper in ecstasy. He overwhelmed her within seconds, flooding her body with undeniable pleasure that kept building, twisting, arcing into…into…

Dear god, she would not give *this* man her orgasm.

Lexie screamed as she came, every part of her vibrating on a frequency her body had never hummed to before. She quivered with each delightful aftershock and groaned when Dane removed his fingers. Lexie became aware of her ragged breathing. She kept her eyes closed and the tears she'd held back earlier threatened to defy her as Dane caressed her cheek.

"What was your mission, Lexie? Tell me now. Or do I have to make you come a few more times?"

Lexie's heart twisted as she forced herself to look up into Dane's handsome face. She could've taken pain, but more treacherous climaxes bestowed by her assassin? "Please, please just kill me." Lexie trembled as a tear slid down her cheek.

Silence stretched between them before Dane cursed, his hard gaze softening. "I'm not going to kill you." He smoothed her hair. "You're one of the best operatives we have."

"I'm not going to talk." Lexie tuned out Dane's voice as she made peace with her fate. She'd done the best job she could. "I won't talk. Take that knife and—" Lexie froze as Dane took hold of her chin.

"Lexie, I'm going to need you to focus now."

Lexie blinked as Dane reached over her. She frowned when he fixed her bra and buttoned up her blouse.

"I was planted here to test you. It happens to all of us at least once." Dane pulled her split skirt down. "I could've used other methods, but I didn't think those would be as effective." He moved out of her line of sight. Lexie felt him undoing the rope around her ankles. Moments later her legs were free. "I will confirm in my report what the company already knows. You're an exemplary, loyal asset."

"I don't believe this," Lexie said as he untied her hands. She sat up and rubbed her wrists.

"It's the truth." Dane put all the rope he'd gathered back into her bag.

Stunned, Lexie watched him pocket her panties as he approached her. Her pulse quickened when she saw evidence of his impressive hard-on.

"Are you all right?"

Lexie stood, glaring up at Dane as he grinned. "I'm fine."

"Good." Dane buttoned his suit jacket. "Because our mark will be here any second."

"Right, Mr. Leland." Lexie grabbed her hair clip from the table. "Wait. *Our* mark?" She pulled her mussed hair back as she looked over Dane's shoulder through the glass facing the hallway.

"I thought if we worked together, got done faster…we could—"

Lexie pressed her finger to Dane's lips. "*Our* mark is here."

TIED AND TWISTED

Jodie Griffin

Tied up, twisted, teased and tormented.

As I watched Mason work, I kept hearing those words in my head. My Master's words, ones he'd whispered in my ear countless times over the past couple of weeks until I couldn't think of anything but him and what he had planned for me. Fucking with my mind while he tortured my body was one of his favorite games.

A few weeks ago, he'd pulled me close, a sexy glint in his eye. As a car pulled into our driveway, he told me he'd planned an adults-only weekend away for us. While footsteps echoed up the flagstone walk, he told me it was, specifically, a weekend of bondage. As the doorbell rang, he whispered his sadistic plans in my ear. I greeted our guests with a red face, hard nipples and soaking wet panties.

The last two weeks had been one elaborate, drawn-out mindfuck of a scene that included a week—*an entire damn week*—of orgasm denial. For me, not for him, and by the time this weekend rolled around I was ready to kill someone.

We'd arrived late yesterday. Kink Kamp ran from Friday night through Sunday at a gated, private campground—one that happened to be the same place where our son went for scout camp during the summer, which was hysterical, but I was trying not to think about that.

Not that you'd ever know it was the same place, looking around the wooded area now. I was on my knees after having been stripped naked by my Master, waiting silently on a quilt at his feet. Around us, there were other blankets, other people in various states of dress and undress, and more rope. Lots and lots of rope, in every color of the rainbow.

There were portable Saint Andrew's crosses, spanking benches, even a metal jungle gym–type setup with hanging hardpoints. And there were huge trees with super-thick branches, strong enough to hold a suspended person.

Mason had just finished securing a suspension ring to one of the really heavy branches, and we were waiting for a camp monitor to come inspect it. Part of the rules of the weekend included safety inspections before any suspensions, but I trusted Mason with my life and I knew it was safe even without one. Right now, he was hanging from it himself, and if it could hold him, it would hold me.

I couldn't keep my eyes off him. His T-shirt was snug against his chest, the muscles of his arms standing out sharply. His jeans rode low on his hips, and he had a day's worth of beard on his face. He looked dark and dangerous and sexy as hell. I was used to seeing him in suit and tie, which really worked for me, but I loved this side of him too.

"You ready, Addie-mine?"

"Yes, Master. *Please.*" I couldn't keep the begging tone out of my voice. I was ready. Just past noon on Saturday and Mason *still* hadn't let me come. He'd fucked my mouth last night out under the stars, come down my throat and aroused me until I'd wanted to cry. *Had* cried, utter frustration winding me tighter and tighter. Then he'd whispered those damned words in my ear again—*tied up, twisted, teased and tormented*—stroking me until my body settled as much as it was going to, and held me close all night while we slept.

This afternoon, the noises around us in the scene areas were intoxicating. We rarely played anywhere but at home, and I'd almost forgotten how other people's play could drive my own arousal up. The sounds of slapping hands and toys against flesh. Moans. Grunts. Fucking. It all spiked my need higher, and I was ready for whatever Mason had in mind. More than ready.

Desperate.

He dropped from the ring, gave it one more yank and let it go, turning his attention fully back to me.

Seared by his hot gaze, I had to bite back a needy sound. Mason just grinned, the sadist.

I loved him for that.

His toy bag was beside me, and he reached in and drew out several long, carefully coiled lengths of rope, laying them on one of those camp chairs beside me. He hooked his finger into the O-ring on my play collar, and drew me to my feet.

I shivered. I'm a rope slut. I love the way it makes me feel confined but safe, trapped but free. My brain works at top speed all the time, the hamster on the wheel constantly running. Eighty million things all at once, every fear I've ever had about our son and our jobs and our life and our marriage, all tied up and twisted together. Mason knows that about me, so maybe he'd chosen those specific words for a reason. *Tied up, twisted, teased and tormented.*

Mason also knows something incredible happens when he binds me with rope. I go elsewhere in my mind, somewhere calm and quiet, the running hamster sound asleep for that all-too-brief period of time. The first time it happened was a revelation. The second time, I was shocked. The third time, I sobbed, scaring the hell out of my husband.

Ropespace. I love it, and Mason knows it.

"Here we go, love. Lift your arms." Mason's low words were murmured. There's not much talking when he's working his magic. He lets me zone out, his touches sure but gentle, his hands directing me where he needs me to go. He began wrapping rope around my body in a harness—my shoulders, my chest, my waist, my hips—and I swayed along with his movements, my eyes closed.

"Fucking beautiful." His words came from behind me and landed in my ear. I smiled, in my happy place. Then he pinched my nipple and bit my neck and I shivered, leaning back against him. His hands continued to touch me, adjusting rope, teasing skin.

I heard him say thank you—to the safety monitor, I guessed—and then he maneuvered me a few steps forward. I still had my eyes closed, but I felt him attach my harness to the suspension ring, then a bunch of tugging as he shifted me horizontal, my feet coming off the ground. He pulled harder and lifted me higher, then tied the ropes off.

I was faceup, floating on air. I let my head drop back and my arms fly to my sides, my bones and muscles shifting to settle within their rope bonds. I gasped as part of the harness, ropes that ran between my legs, came to rest in the crack of my ass. The knot Mason had tied in them was at exactly the right spot to press against the fat plug he'd teased and tortured into my ass this morning.

It felt so damn good to be outside, naked, swinging from a tree in a very adult, very kinky twist on a favorite pastime.

September was the perfect time for this. It wasn't too hot out, and most of the mosquitoes were gone. The sun was warm on my body, as a light breeze ruffled the leaves on the trees.

Mason bent my leg and wrapped rope around my thigh and calf, binding them together. Apparently I wasn't going to be allowed to simply fly free today. My muscles screamed for a moment, but when he finished the tie, they relaxed. He moved to the other leg, doing the same. This time, though, he tied it off to the ring, so one bent leg was up, while the other was hanging down, not suspended by anything but gravity. Air blew against my core, making me shiver, and then I realized it was Mason, not a warm late-summer breeze. He licked me until I thought I'd lose my mind, twisted the butt plug and then, when I groaned, bit the inside of my thigh.

His hands coasted over my skin, between my legs, inside my body, touching me as though he had every right to—and he did. I'd given him that right the day I'd accepted his collar, and again when we'd said our wedding vows. I loved it, more than I'd ever be able to describe to anyone. Mere words couldn't measure what being dominated by my Master did for me.

The bite of the rope and the scratch of his skin melded into one long stream of sensation, but he still wasn't done. Again he worked silently, allowing me time to bask in the quiet in my head. He cuffed my wrists together behind me with more rope, then tied them to the leg that was hanging free.

I heard murmurs around me but they were just white noise. I was focused on the touch of Mason's hands. I let out a gasp when his mouth sucked hard at my nipple. He clamped one and I groaned. He laughed and did the other, then tied them off to the suspension ring, tugging at the clamps, causing a delicious ache between my thighs. I made some noises but couldn't form any words to beg him to stop—or do it harder.

I'm not sure how long Mason let me drift there, but it was long enough for my mind to empty of clutter. It was a gift of time from my Master, the one man who knew every chaotic inch of my heart, body, mind and soul.

I felt free and safe and loved.

Soon other things began to filter in, though I was still floating in ropespace. Mason's hands supporting my head, his thumbs brushing my cheeks. "Open, baby," he murmured in his deep, deep voice. I did, and he pushed his cock inside, gliding against my tongue. I licked him and sucked, but a flick of the rope attached to the nipple clamp had me moaning.

He bent over me, whispering in my ear in a singsong way. "Mason's got Addie strung up from a tree, they're f-u-c-k-i-n-g." On each letter, he took the opportunity to withdraw and plunge deep, pushing into my throat. I was at exactly the right angle to ease his way, and each time he pressed into me it jiggled the nipple clamps, making me gasp around his erection.

Need unfurled inside me, drawing me out of ropespace and back into the moment. I peeled my eyes open, blinking at the bright sun beaming through the leaves of the tree above me. "Please, Master! I need to come. *Oh, please.*"

"Not quite yet, my sweet little slut." He kissed me, then nipped my chin. "I asked Master Silas to join us for this part, and you're going to let him hold you if you need it. Got it?"

"Yes, Master." Silas was Mason's mentor and he'd assisted in scenes before when Mason needed another set of hands for my safety. I trusted him and, more importantly, Mason trusted him with me. I belong to my Master, and no one fucks me but him. Silas would never cross that line, but that didn't mean Mason didn't like seeing and I didn't enjoy having another man's hands on me.

Mason let go of my head and it dropped back again. My

vision upside down, I saw Master Silas step forward until my eyes were nearly even with his groin. He bent over and looked in my eyes. "Hey there, sweetness." He grinned and flicked the rope attached to my nipple clamps. I groaned. "A little worked up, are we?"

Another damn sadist. "Yes, Sir."

He slipped his hands under my head and neck, the same way Mason had. "Too bad he won't share you this way. I'd love to fuck your mouth in this position while he fucks your pussy. It looked damned hot from where I was watching."

His voice was rough and his body aroused, but he didn't make any moves to unzip his pants. Part of me—the still denied part of me—considered begging Mason to allow it, but that was a bridge I wasn't sure I was comfortable crossing. As it was, my one-track mind and my attention were yanked away from temptation when Mason grabbed my hips and surged into me with one long, hard thrust.

I screamed and arched my back, my head pressing down against Silas's hands. "Master!"

"Lift her up, Si, before she hurts herself. Feel free to play with her tits."

Silas maneuvered me so my head was no longer hanging down and my shoulders were leaning against his chest, his hands cupping my breasts. He squeezed them and I gritted my teeth against the shocking pain as Mason thrust into me again.

Silas bit my ear, then whispered into it. "Look at him, Addie. Look at his face. He's as much yours as you are his. If I tried to fuck your mouth, he'd rip my damn head off. The little one first, and then the big one."

I started to laugh but Mason fucked into me again and I cried out instead.

Together, they set a rhythm that had me gasping and shaking

and panting. Silas would tug at the nipple clamps and Mason would power into me, sending my nerves into overdrive.

"Oh god, I need to come. Please may I come? Please, Master?" My mind was spinning, my body tight with denied release. I hovered on the edge of something amazing, and I wasn't sure how much more I could take. My eyes filled with tears and spilled over. "Please."

"Come for me," Mason ordered, fucking me hard, his fingers gripping my hips so tightly I knew I'd have bruises. Heat and pressure built inside me, but I couldn't get there, even though he'd told me I could.

I started begging. "Please, please, please, please."

"Now, Silas," Mason growled. Silas removed the nipple clamps as Mason fucked me, pinching my clit.

I shrieked at the pain and the pleasure, flying off the precipice into a roiling sea. Mason came with a shout to match mine. Breathing heavily, he held me as close as he could, his head bowed forward.

I felt Silas press a kiss to my temple as he released the ropes keeping me suspended. He helped Mason carry me to the blanket where they set me down on my stomach.

"Thanks, man," Mason murmured, and with my head turned sideways, I saw Silas leave us alone again.

Carefully, Mason unbound my arms. As they were released I groaned, feeling the ache in them. He rubbed my shoulders and pressed a kiss between them, along my spine. I was still breathing heavily from my release, and slightly sore from the suspension, but I felt languid and loose too. That had been one hell of an orgasm.

He left the harness on but removed the ropes binding my legs, and again, I groaned. His hands felt wonderful as he massaged my legs, his fingers digging into the overstretched muscles. When he finished they were limp noodles. If I had to get up and run, I'd be in big trouble. My heart was a tumble of emotions, my mind still mostly filled with cotton.

Mason stretched out next to me on the quilt and pulled me into his arms. He kissed me, then tucked my head under his chin, pulling a thin blanket over me. "I love you, Addie-mine. You please me very much. Rest now. We've got more to do later. So much more." He murmured nonsense words to me, stroking my skin with gentle hands.

"I love you too." I closed my eyes, knowing I was safe and protected in my Master's embrace.

COCOON

Annabeth Leong

Ruby had never been in bondage so complex that it required coolant. As Paula wound tubing around her body and taped it in place, Ruby's stomach dropped in that familiar, exhilarating, maybe-this-isn't-such-a-great-idea-after-all sort of way.

Except that this wasn't familiar at all. Ruby had never played in Paula's basement before. The gymnastics mat beneath her felt sticky and spongy under her bare toes. The acrid smell of industrial cling wrap filled the place, and the lighting was weird.

She hadn't played with Paula that much, either—just a few times, until Ruby had been sure that she felt safe enough to get extreme with her.

No matter how many times Ruby had brought herself off to pictures of people wrapped tight until they couldn't move at all, and no matter how many times her clit had pulsed to thoughts of full-body heat and constriction, there was nothing familiar about the reality of it. Paula had explained exactly what they were going to do, and Ruby had nodded politely through that conversation and then gone home to masturbate furiously, but when it came down to it, she still felt as if she had no understanding of what was about to happen to her.

Ruby began to tremble.

Paula patted her absently on the hip but continued her task. She clinked as she moved, and Ruby wondered what was making that sound. The medical tape she used to attach the tubing to Ruby's inner thighs itched. "Do we need so much of that?"

Paula glanced up at her with an inscrutable expression. "You're going to want it once I get you covered in plastic, sweetie. I don't want our scene to end early because you're overheating."

Covered in plastic. The words echoed through Ruby's head. She imagined her skin compressed, sweaty, suffocating under layer upon layer of cling wrap. The misery and the helplessness attached to the image made her squirm and press her thighs together, dislodging a length of tubing and earning her a light slap from Paula. Ruby had never been able to explain why it got her so hot to picture herself so unhappy, and then she'd met Paula, who didn't care why.

Her teeth chattered.

Paula cocked her head. "We can stop if you need to. I could play with just your hands or something, not your whole body. I know this is a big step for you."

Ruby spent a moment wishing that Paula would be meaner. If she would cackle like a villain and tell Ruby that she was trapped in the dungeon now and had no choice, this might be easier. It felt particularly humiliating to have to look her in the eye and admit, "No, I want to do this. Please don't stop." People often talked as if BDSM was about doing a favor to the top—"submitting" to dominance, "letting" her spank you. Since Ruby had turned fantasy to reality, she had learned an uncomfortable truth. Paula was doing her a favor. She was spending money, time and skill putting on an elaborate scene for Ruby's benefit, because Ruby needed to feel confined, because Ruby wanted to get off. It was hard enough to ask people for simple things, and harder still to ask for complicated, extreme, slightly dangerous things. Ruby's stomach flipped over as she recalled seeking Paula out because of the magic word "mummification" listed on her kinky social network profile. She suspected that she needed Paula more than Paula needed her.

By the time Ruby worked that all out in her head, Paula had already nodded and finished attaching her tubing. "Let me test this," she muttered, adjusting Ruby as if she were a recalcitrant piece of machinery. Paula picked up the bucket of ice water she'd prepared earlier, her stout body showing no sign of effort. She grinned as she raised it to the level of Ruby's head, her broad nose flattening as her face widened. "Get ready. Try not to move."

She inserted one end of Ruby's tubing into the water, and after a few moments, gravity began to make the siphon work. An icy sensation curled around Ruby's torso, arms and legs as the cold water traveled through the tubing and into the bucket waiting at the other end. Ruby shrieked. She fanned her hands against the outsides of her thighs, trying to hold still as Paula had commanded, but needing some sort of outlet for her reaction to the cold.

Paula grunted. "You'll thank me for this later, believe me." She paused. "Though you might also scream twice as loud as that."

She lowered the bucket, leaving Ruby gasping.

Before Ruby could recover, Paula reached into her pants pocket and pulled out a handful of pennies. She taped them in evenly spaced rows over Ruby's body.

"What are those for?"

Paula raised an eyebrow. "I explained this the day we had coffee. They're for making vents. In case I need to let your skin breathe."

However, she offered no additional explanation for the coins that went over Ruby's hard nipples, nor for the special rigging that allowed her to position a quarter over Ruby's arousal-slicked clit. Ruby looked down at her body, which already looked strange thanks to the medical tape, and decided not to press Paula to tell her more. She liked to be restricted more than she liked to submit, but she saw no need to be a brat when Paula was going to so much trouble.

Paula attached a last piece of medical tape with a flourish, then thumped Ruby's ass with her palm. "There. Now we're ready for the real fun." She rushed to her racks of industrial cling wrap with a sort of manic enthusiasm that put Ruby paradoxically at ease. Paula was enjoying herself, too.

She returned with a tube of plastic wrap as long as her torso tucked under one arm and two rolls of duct tape swinging off her outstretched fingers. She seemed lighter on her feet and much less stolid.

Before Paula started in with the cling wrap, she leaned her forehead against Ruby's. "You promised, but I need to make sure. You're going to tell me how you're feeling while we do this, right? Even things that seem trivial to you might be something I need to know. Don't hold back, okay?"

Ruby forced herself to nod.

"Let's practice," Paula coached. "What are you feeling right now?"

"Um..." Ruby wasn't shy with herself, but it was still hard for her to tell other people how kinky she was. "Nervous. Excited." Her voice dropped to a whisper. "Wet."

"Good," Paula purred. She dropped the duct tape at Ruby's feet and used her thumb to work the loose end of the cling wrap off the roll. Accompanied by an exuberant ripping sound, she spread her arms wide, freeing a broad expanse of clear plastic. Paula stepped behind Ruby and hugged her through the cling wrap. In the process, she made a loose tube around Ruby's torso.

Ruby frowned, feeling the wrapping already slipping down her body. She moved her arms apart to hold it in place, but Paula pushed them down against her sides. "Don't worry," she whispered. "It'll get tighter as we go."

The sound of cling wrap separating from the roll filled Paula's basement, cracking and echoing against the concrete walls. Paula held the roll steady and commanded Ruby to spin into it, forcing her to participate in her own mummification. Ruby obeyed, her movements becoming increasingly awkward as, layer upon layer, the plastic began to squeeze tight around her. She wobbled, dizzy and full of adrenaline.

Paula laughed. "I haven't even done your legs. Don't fall down yet!"

Ruby bit her lip and struggled to continue spinning. A bead of sweat formed inside her armpit then rolled down her arm. It tickled as it traveled but, encased in the plastic, she couldn't do anything about it.

She stopped moving, aware on a visceral level of how helpless she was becoming. Her arms could only wiggle a few millimeters, and Paula had just gotten started.

Paula noticed and responded at once. She stroked Ruby's hair. "How are you feeling?"

Ruby swallowed. "Scared." She corrected herself. "Terrified."

"Fun terrified? Or I-want-to-use-my-safeword-but-I-can't-remember-it terrified?"

Ruby considered the question. "I don't want to use my safeword," she said after a moment.

"Okay. Do you want me to slow down?"

"I want to stop spinning. I feel too off balance."

Paula kissed the top of her ear. "Thank you for saying so." She paused, then pulled Ruby firmly. "Come here."

In the corner was a sturdy pole. Paula pushed Ruby toward it. "This will help you stay on your feet," she said. Ruby nodded. The pole did feel comforting against her back. She no longer felt as if she were going to tumble off her feet or spin into the concrete wall. On the other hand, Paula began to include the pole in the wrapping, pulling Ruby's body straight and taut.

Ruby's torso felt thick and stiff. She tried a few experiments and found she could no longer bend at the waist—not forward, and not side to side either. No rope or restraint had ever immobilized her abdominals. It was an odd feeling, as if the pole behind her had replaced her spine.

"Keep talking to me," Paula murmured. Her wraps had begun to travel lower, down over Ruby's hips and the tops of her thighs. Ruby felt a sudden urge to resist her immobilization and tried to spread her legs. Paula didn't fight her, but the wraps pulled her knees closer together inexorably, a millimeter at a time.

Ruby scanned her body, trying to obey Paula's command. Her heart pounded. She couldn't seem to relax, and she'd become aware that the more desperate her body became to free itself, the faster blood pumped through her body, and the hotter she got. She noticed that she felt sticky underneath the plastic, clammy and uncomfortable, especially in the places where her skin made contact with the metal coins.

"It doesn't feel good," she admitted to Paula. "I'm at the point where I think this isn't very fun after all. I sort of want to stop. I don't like the plastic. I don't like the way it's squeezing me. I don't like that I can't get out."

Paula laughed again, patting Ruby's side affectionately. Her touch seemed distant through the layers of plastic, muffled and awkward. Ruby shivered, reminded yet again of how constrained she was. "I love this part," she whispered, a new and vicious tone entering her voice. "There's no pretending now. You couldn't work your way out of this if you tried. And it feels miserable. You're too hot. You're totally helpless. And unless you use that safeword after all, there's absolutely nothing you can do about it. The plastic is going to get tighter and tighter. Your temperature's going to keep rising. You can curse me, beg me, whatever you like, but there's nowhere at all that you can go. You can't adjust yourself. Not even slightly." She stepped closer, her hands resting on Ruby's plastic-covered hips. "I'm going to blindfold you and wait until I can tell that you've decided you hate it. That's when I'll play with you. I have ways of making your clit so big and hard you can't stand it, but your thighs will be clamped together so your juices won't be able to drip down. They'll just collect in your cunt, and you'll realize that, not only do you hate this, you're more aroused than you've ever been, and there's nothing you can do about that either."

Ruby's eyes widened. She'd been on the verge of using her safeword, but Paula's speech made her clit pulse so hard she could feel it in the back of her eyes. She whimpered. Paula brushed her lips against Ruby's jaw, and though Ruby flinched away with her head, her body could not follow. She could no more retreat from Paula than she could approach her.

Paula grinned, her glee giving Ruby a clearer sense of what she enjoyed about mummifying a submissive. Then she continued to wind plastic around Ruby's legs. "Keep telling me how uncomfortable you are," she ordered.

Ruby squeezed her eyes shut and did her best. "It's sweaty under the plastic. I swear it's fifteen degrees hotter under here. My circulation's getting a little weird. My fingertips are tingling."

Paula paused. "Yeah?" She felt the pulse in Ruby's neck and several spots on her legs that were still exposed. "I think you're okay, but keep me posted on that."

Ruby nodded. Paula had shown her the medical shears attached to her belt loop, but Ruby realized now that she hoped there would be no need to use them. "This is really unpleasant, but I don't want you to cut me out just yet," Ruby said, thinking she ought to voice the thought out loud.

"Tell me why I shouldn't."

"I need it to be a little bit unpleasant."

"Why?" Paula had finished with the cling wrap. Now she was sealing her work off with duct tape.

"I don't really know," Ruby admitted. "I just know that's the part that turns me on. And it's the part I can't do for myself. I don't have enough willpower to hold still if I get myself into an uncomfortable situation."

"Well, you're going to hold still now," Paula declared. It was true. Ruby was cocooned in plastic, the wrapping so thick that it obscured the details of her naked body. Until the medical shears released her, Paula's handiwork confined her to the tiniest twitches. "And I'm going to make you less comfortable, but safer." She retrieved her buckets.

"Oh no," Ruby said. "Please."

"I told you, we have to make sure you don't overheat." Beside the pole, above the level of Ruby's head, was a little shelf that Paula must have built expressly for her siphon. She hefted the bucket of ice water onto it.

What had been merely cold before was an inescapable

freezing grasp now. Ruby screamed so loudly that she felt her uvula vibrating. For the first time, she truly struggled against the plastic that held her and discovered how implacable it was. Another powerful throb went through her clit. It wasn't quite an orgasm, but the spasm left her gasping.

Paula laid a hand over Ruby's stomach. "Your helpless little wriggles are so sweet," she said with a wicked smile.

Ruby couldn't stand the chill in contrast to the sticky heat under the plastic. "I think you're evil," she sobbed, still squirming uselessly.

"I'm definitely evil," Paula grinned. "Now, how else am I going to play with you?"

Ruby tried to get used to the wild variations of temperature under the plastic, but she felt completely off balance. The skin of her forehead was clammy with sweat. Paula approached with a roll of cloth bandages. "We need to cover your eyes," she said. "I want you to lose all sense of time. You're going to have no idea how long I've kept you like this, completely immobilized, sobbing for me, at my mercy."

Ruby opened her mouth, but no sound came out. Paula's words filled her with horror and dread. Right on the heels of those terrible feelings, however, was utter, overwhelming arousal. Ruby wanted to beg, but she didn't know for what.

The cloth began to wind around her head, covering her eyes in meticulous layers that gradually shut out her view of the basement. "Was this what you thought it would be like?" Paula whispered. Her rough voice seemed to scratch Ruby's ear.

"It's more," Ruby told her.

"Good. Remember, we're still just getting started."

Then Paula stepped back, and Ruby couldn't feel her anymore. Ruby's jaw worked for a moment. She was hot, uncomfortable, abandoned and scared. Her cunt twitched again, but she couldn't give herself over to arousal without a little reassurance. "Paula?" The sound was small.

"I'm right here. I'm just going to let you stew in that for a minute. I like watching you trapped like an insect in a spiderweb."

Paula's image brought up old fantasies for Ruby. She remembered her vivid and confused reactions to damsels in distress in old movies, attached to train tracks with coiled ropes. She thought of spies strapped down to chairs and interrogated. More than these common fantasies, though, Ruby had always been struck by butterflies struggling to free themselves from cocoons, people stuck in quicksand, and one movie in which a hotshot starship pilot had been encased inside a solid block of an unyielding mineral. That total and complete imprisonment had always awakened her deepest longings. Immobilized by Paula's plastic, Ruby's heart seemed to beat from her clit.

She was still uncomfortable in her bondage. Her body froze and burned. Now, however, Paula's other promise came true. Deep and undeniable arousal stirred in the depths of Ruby's cunt, and she was completely helpless to satisfy it. Knowing she could do nothing made her feel it even more.

Soon, though she knew it was futile, she was fighting the plastic as hard as she could, grunting and raising her body temperature, squeezing her inner muscles, desperate to grip anything at all.

Ruby had no idea how long her private battle went on. At some point, metal scraped on metal and there was pressure over her left nipple. Then that sensitive flesh was somehow horribly and miraculously bare.

She felt as if she'd grown more nerves while inside the plastic. Even the air stimulated her nipple beyond endurance. A fingernail skimmed its tip, and Ruby screamed as if she'd been ripped in two. "What the—? How are you—?" She spluttered, unable to collect herself enough to demand an explanation.

Paula pinched the nipple, making Ruby howl. "This is one of my favorite tricks," she said. "Those coins I taped to your body let me cut through the plastic without hurting you. It means I can get access to the spots I want to play with."

As Ruby absorbed this information, there were two smart strokes over her right nipple, and then that flesh, too, was yanked out of the plastic cocoon.

A tear fell from Ruby's eye but was absorbed by the bandages before it could trace a path down her cheek. She couldn't decide whether her raw, sensitive nipples were hungry to be touched or desperate to be left alone, but that didn't matter because they were Paula's playthings now. When Paula flicked them, Ruby could not so much as jerk.

She panted, gasped and grunted. Her body was absolutely restrained, but her voice had been unleashed. She made unhinged noises when Paula scraped her teeth over the tips of her nipples, and she wailed like an otherworldly being when Paula fished some ice out of her bucket and pressed it pitilessly against Ruby's chest.

"How do you feel?" Paula asked once more. Ruby could still hear the concerned inquiry of a good top, but they had both gotten lost in the scene, and the question had a decidedly sadistic twist as well. "Do you like being helpless like this? Wrapped tight like a mummy? Unable to pull back even a centimeter?" Her voice dropped to a whisper. "Does it make you horny?"

"Yes," Ruby sobbed. It made her desperately horny. She had masturbated to this fantasy a hundred times, but the reality, in all its glorious discomfort and overpowering sensation, turned her imagined impressions into dull shadows.

"I can make you come," Paula said, tweaking Ruby's nipples

for emphasis, "but it's probably going to hurt. Do you want me to?"

Ruby thought of the quarter over her clit with a shudder. If she felt the same wild nerve signals in her clit that she had in her nipples, she thought she might lose her mind. She couldn't resist, though. A part of her *wanted* to lose her mind. "Please do it," she told Paula.

"If you say so."

Under the plastic, Ruby shuddered. Her teeth chattered. Her nipples seemed to throb and grow larger with each beat of her heart. They had become obscene, swollen fruit ripe for Paula's taking, and her clit was about to be the same.

Paula cut the quarter free and blew on Ruby's revealed clit. The humidity of her breath felt like a hundred thousand jets of water shot at Ruby's engorged flesh with force. Every muscle in Ruby's body tensed uselessly. "I changed my mind!" she cried. "I don't think I can take it!" She knew that Paula was about to lick her clit, and she thought of the rough, complicated surface of a tongue and knew that it would obliterate her newly awakened nerve endings.

"Are you changing your mind with a safeword?"

Ruby could hear the smile in Paula's voice. She knew as well as Ruby that there was no turning back. After fantasizing about mummification all her life, Ruby was too curious to back away from its extremes. "No," Ruby whispered. "Not with a safeword."

"Then you're saying you want me to lick this hard little clit even though you know it's going to feel like ice and fire rolled into one."

Ruby hung her head. "Yes," she whispered. "That's what I'm saying." Paula's care and solicitousness had begun to seem meaner than the cruelest insults a top could throw. She never let

Ruby off the hook. She always made Ruby take full responsibility for the things she wanted done to her.

"Then say it for me," Paula ordered.

Blinded, desperate, hot, sweaty, tingling, Ruby felt as if the only parts of her body that really existed were the parts that Paula had exposed. The lower half of her face, her neck, her nipples, her feet and her clit. They all pulsed in the harsh open air. "Please," Ruby said. "Please lick my clit even though it's going to hurt like hell."

Paula did as Ruby asked. The flat of her tongue rolled up Ruby's confused clit, and it was velvet, it was pinpricks, it was lightning, it was ocean, it was flooding Ruby, it was killing her. It was making her come.

The orgasm slashed and burned through Ruby's captive body. She had almost no other sensations to distract her from it. There was a sound she didn't recognize until she figured out that it was a raw scream torn from the purest, deepest part of her.

One stroke of Paula's tongue shattered Ruby inside her cocoon. Only the plastic was holding her together. She sagged, though that did not change her position much.

Beneath her, Paula waited, and Ruby wondered for a moment if she could take another lick of the unholy fire of her tongue. Perhaps another time, Ruby thought. If Paula wanted to do this again.

In a small, reverent voice, Ruby whispered her safeword, because safety and comfort were what she needed now. Paula responded at once, holding her, finding a spot to start in with the shears.

"You're a good girl," she whispered. "A brave girl."

Tears leaked from Ruby's eyes, but they were different now, cleaner. This had been Ruby's most extreme fantasy, and trying it with Paula had moved the horizon of her imagination back and made her world feel larger. Though still wrapped in the plastic, Ruby felt as if she had entered a more expansive place. She wanted to travel more unexplored territory with Paula, who knew so many cruel tricks and was also so careful and good. They could talk about that later. Now, Ruby closed her eyes as Paula gradually pulled her out of her cocoon and reintroduced her to the world.

AUCTION, IN QUOTATION MARKS

LN Bey

Mike was mortified at being the only male slave in the auction. It made it even more humbling, more emasculating than if there were another. He stood naked on the stage but for his leather collar, two nude women to the right of him, one astonishingly beautiful brunette to his left, too proud to speak to the likes of him. Another woman was standing out in front of this line of naked people, in the bright lights. She was the second to be sold. The first was already gone.

Of course, this wasn't a *real* slave auction. It was a social construct, an agreement made by everyone in the room to behave in a certain way. Mike could turn and leave at any moment.

But he didn't.

He kept his place in the line, this wall of otherwise female flesh. Leaving would involve raising quite a commotion, drawing even more attention to himself. He had no idea where his clothes were, and the metal loops in his padlocked collar were attached by thin chains to the collars on either side of him, keeping everyone close together—so close he could smell their scents.

"Twenty-two thousand dollars," said the auctioneer, a short man in a suit behind a podium. A tall brunette dolled up in stiletto boots and black dominatrix regalia walked up to the naked girl center stage, attached a leash to her collar, and led her away.

Mike wasn't sure where the money from this event went, since they weren't really property. He'd gathered this was some sort of charity event, possibly for a local animal shelter. He knew this wasn't the wealthiest crowd in town, like the people who made up the owners/Masters in most erotic novels and stories—characters who could afford exclusive mansions, private islands, even castles, global networks of slave training and trading.

No, these were west-side suburban McMansioners, kinksters who could afford to have some fun, lease a downtown ballroom to rent out their play-slaves for the weekend, but not import the latest beauty by private jet for their harem or stable. They owned car dealerships, not hedge funds. They drove Lexuses and Audis, not Rolls Royces or Bugattis. He knew the type. His Mistress was one.

"Sold to number seventy-seven," the man said. That many people were here? He felt even more nervous and ridiculous.

The dominatrix returned and unhooked the next girl, a petite redhead, from the end of the line, and led her up to the center of the stage. The dominatrix became a game-show showgirl, holding her arms toward the slave, palms up, as though she were a new car.

"Next up is Janella, if you'll check your sale bill," the auctioneer said. Sale bill? Really? "Yes, she is a natural redhead. Too bad they shaved her, eh? Bidding starts at five thousand dollars."

Mike had never been on such display with anyone but his Mistress, except for one weekend when she'd had a friend in from out of town. He'd had to make them drinks, serve them food, be her guest's footstool. It was thrilling. But this was different—public, impersonal.

The worst part of tonight had been the opening hour, when all the buyers were served drinks, and the six slaves had to hold perfectly still so the prospective bidders could look them over close up.

Not just look. They were lined up against one wall of the ballroom and told to stand with their hands behind their heads, elbows back, their legs spread as wide as possible. The buyers made the rounds, cocktails in their hands.

He was told to open his mouth wide for them, bend over as far as he could. He was pinched and prodded, his balls squeezed and slapped, his cock pulled and handled, brought to embarrassing erection more than once. At least he was never penetrated.

The most embarrassing thing was when people just talked to him, especially the men. He could see the amusement and confused derision on their faces, and they would ask him questions, getting increasingly intoxicated. "Look at her, next to you," one man said, gray-haired and starting to slur. He pointed his glass at the gorgeous and splayed brunette beside him. "You should be *fuckin'* her, not standing there naked yourself. What are ya, queer or somethin'?"

"No, Sir," was all Mike could say. He had never been with another man, had never wanted to.

Why had his Mistress thought this would be fun? Did she think he needed more training, more experience? Which novel was that, where the Master sent the girl off to be trained and sold, expecting to get her back?

"We're only going to do this once, but her Master wants you to hear it," the auctioneer said. The dominatrix was holding a long rattan cane. She placed her hand gently on the redhead's hip and whispered into her ear, and the girl raised her arms. With no hesitation or warning, the dominatrix swung the cane and struck the girl hard across the ass, causing her to cry out in the sweetest, saddest cry of pain and desire and—was that betrayal?—that Mike had ever heard. Had the girls before her been whipped? He just couldn't concentrate.

"Nice, eh?" The auctioneer said. The dominatrix turned her around to show the audience the marking. Mike's heart sped up and he felt a stirring in his cock as he saw her pained expression. "She has agreed to spend her entire two-week vacation with whoever buys her. Think of it—twenty-four hours a day, two weeks. You could grow that little red bush back, in that much time. Ownership reverts to her Master once she returns to her waitressing job." Wow. Mike only had the weekend to spare. The thought of submitting, full time, to someone for two full weeks—it was something his Mistress had never asked of him. It was an intoxicating idea, an amazing fantasy.

The audience felt the same way. Mike could make out hands being raised, and the auctioneer was suddenly very busy counting. "Forty-eight thousand dollars," he said, slamming his gavel. "Sold to number fifteen." She was led by the leather-clad woman off the stage, and the dominatrix took the next woman off the line.

Mike's Mistress wasn't really his Mistress. Sandra was someone who had dominant sex with him, with varying levels of enthusiasm. He'd met her at the café where he worked. Dates during the week were just dates, with her wanting to blow off steam about work, followed by straight sex.

Saturdays were different. Saturdays approximated his fantasies. She was In Charge. He would show up Friday night, and was expected to strip at the door. He would serve her all the next day, a very one-sided pampering, both in bed and out. She had toys, little whips.

But some Saturdays, once he'd gotten her off (always orally, at first), she would loosen up, relax. Tell him to just lie on the bed and watch TV with her, sometimes naked and still frustrated, sometimes telling him to put a robe on.

"Go ahead and call me Sandra," she'd say.

The game was usually over, at that point, the illusion shattered.

It was hard work, she'd tell him, always having to think of something for him to do. Sometimes, she said, she just didn't want the responsibility.

He didn't love her, but he was devoted to her.

He remembered a story he'd read about a male secretary who'd interviewed for an extremely demanding boss, who wanted him at her beck and call day *and* night—he totally gave himself to her. How thrilling that level of submission and demand would be.

So today, his Mistress had told him to strip, and she had shaved his entire body, except for a patch of pubic hair above his cock. She'd waxed between his legs—very painful. But she was loving, gentle, admiring of his body. He *was* in good shape. She gave him a little massage.

Then she said, "I'm going to auction you off. Get dressed."

"What? When?" he'd asked.

"Right now."

But this wasn't at all what Mike had pictured. He'd imagined, once he'd realized she was serious, a half-dozen women in her living room, a sort of girls' night in, drinks and laughs, with him serving as the entertainment. She *had* shared him, once. Sort of like having a stripper over, but there would be token cash and the winner would lead him by a leash into the guest room. Or, more in line with his longtime fantasies, he'd have to service each of the women, in front of the others on his hands and knees, kissing feet and licking cunts, being laughed at as he crawled his way around the room.

But that kind of thing just didn't happen. Then again, neither did this.

It's all about expectations, isn't it? Reality never quite jibed with the fantasy. So often it's a letdown, but sometimes it's... this?

The dominatrix—the auctioneer had finally called her Mistress Anna—whispered into the girl's ear. This woman, a blonde with fair skin and magnificent breasts, spread her feet wide, exposing herself to the audience, and cupped her hands under her boobs, lifting them, offering them.

Mistress Anna now held a riding crop, much shorter than the rattan cane, and after a smiling gesture along the girl's body, struck her hard across her presented breasts. Behind her, Mike watched her bare back as she flinched and cried out.

"This is Sheila," the auctioneer announced. Mistress Anna struck her chest again, and again she cried. "Sheila's limits give the buyer a little more leeway in the pain department," he said. "She likes the whip."

Mike tried to think of something boring. This was going to be too much. He didn't know any baseball statistics, the old cliché, so he tried to think of old Top 40 charts from his youth. It wasn't working.

Mistress Anna struck Sheila's breasts again, and again. Mike tried to think of the old hit songs, but he could only picture how red Sheila's fabulous tits must be getting, with their fair skin and light pink nipples.

Sheila's cries were beginning to meld into one nonstop moan. Mike could hear anxious murmurs behind the stage lights as Anna kept up her whipping.

What had been a slight thickening of Mike's cock during Janella's sale was now a raging hard-on, and his face was surely as red as Sheila's tits up there in center stage. That's another reason it was so embarrassing being the only man—he was the only one whose excitement was on full display.

"Sheila is available for a three-day weekend, before she has to return to work," the auctioneer said over the sound of leather against flesh, and there was a collective groan of disappointment from the crowd. "Oh come on now," he said. "Think of just how intense those three days could be!" More slaps, and Sheila's moans got even louder.

"Shall we start the bidding at five thousand?" Sheila was whimpering now, and Mike's cock was rock hard. Mike glanced at the brunette beside him, but in true ice-queen fashion she ignored him.

"Oh come on, now, look at her," the auctioneer pleaded. "She's beautiful. She craves the whip. A shorter stay, but oh, what a weekend it would be. Four thousand, anyone?" He nodded to Mistress Anna, and she stepped back from the panting blonde. "Gentlemen? Ladies?"

He nodded again, and Mistress Anna took a step forward, and, altering her swing, struck the leather flap of the crop squarely against Sheila's shaved crotch, causing her to cry out anew, in a fresh, sharper sound.

She didn't whip as hard, but the sound of the leather hitting between Sheila's spread thighs sent chills through Mike's body, his cock throbbing, his imagination soaring. Sheila stood still, her hands still offering her breasts, face up and now visibly sobbing.

Someone raised his hand. "Four thousand!" the auctioneer said, pointing into the darkness beyond the lights. "Do I hear forty-five? Forty-four?"

More slaps against poor Sheila's cunt. "Forty-four! Do I hear forty-five. Listen to those screams, folks. That could be yours! Forty-five! Forty-six?"

Sheila's body was quivering, shaking from her sobs, but she stayed put.

Mistress Anna stopped her whipping, looked out toward the audience. She reached to Sheila's upheld breast and wiped her finger across it. She held it up to the crowd, wet from Sheila's tears, and placed her finger in her own mouth, tasting it. She seductively drew the finger from her lips. She lowered her hand to Sheila's crotch, and showed her finger to the crowd again. It was glistening wet. Now she licked it, tongue extended, not taking it into her mouth this time. She stepped behind Sheila, and whipped her across her ass, hard, harder than she'd whipped either her tits or cunt. Sheila cried out accordingly, a loud, open-mouthed moan, with her hands still supporting her breasts.

"It's five or nothing, ladies and gentlemen," the auctioneer said, and hands went up. "Five! Do I hear fifty-five hundred?"

"Oh, look," a woman's voice had said during the presale reception. He had been told to keep his eyes lowered, and never speak unless asked a question. His balls ached from the handling, and his cock was still swollen. The voice was familiar. "I know you," she said.

"His name is Michael, the sale bill says," a man's voice said. Mike was looking down at their shoes—nice but not ridiculously expensive. As if he knew.

The woman's hand reached under his chin and lifted. "You're Mike, from the coffee shop," she said. "You know Mike, dear.

The barista who always makes the little hearts in the foam. Tries extra hard, to please." She smiled.

"Oh, yeah. Hey, Mike." Mike was blushing intensely. He'd *really* hoped he wouldn't run into anyone he knew, here.

"Hello, Sir," he said. He knew them. The Millers. They looked like the couples in the erectile dysfunction commercials—Carl was graying but in great shape, "robust"—Barbara younger, though older than Mike, and very attractive, no gray in her reddish brown hair. They were both always elegantly dressed, and friendly to him when he handed them their lattes.

Barbara looked Mike up and down. Jesus, how could he ever face them again at the café?

"He could be our...what was the name of that prince in those first novels we read? The trilogy, in the castle."

"The French one was the first one I ever read," Carl said. "You showed me that trilogy when we started dating." Now he looked down at Mike's naked body, at his cock still half-hard. "If I remember, that prince got it up the ass pretty often," he said.

Mike closed his eyes tight, then remembered being told never to do that. He lowered his eyes, as he'd been told to do. But Barbara lifted his chin again, forcing him to look at them.

"How are things down at the coffee shop, Michael?" she asked.

He could barely speak. "Fine, Ma'am."

"Mm-hm. Do you get medical there?"

"What?" He caught himself. "Ma'am?"

"Medical benefits?"

She must be joking. But he kept it simple:

"No, Ma'am."

"Thirteen thousand," the auctioneer said. "I'm very disappointed, people. She's gorgeous, takes a licking, and this *is* for charity." He waited. "Sold to number twenty-seven." Apparently the buyers wanted longer commitments, something besides a play date. Mistress Anna led Sheila, pale and whipped red, off the stage.

Oh god, no. Mistress Anna walked up to Mike, hips swaying, faint smile on her lips. She unhooked his chain from the goddess next to him, the last slave in waiting. Mike understood, now—the level of abuse increased with each slave, and the staggeringly beautiful woman to his left was going to be the main attraction. He was the final warm-up act.

Mistress Anna didn't leash him: she pulled downward, hard, forcing him onto his knees. "Crawl," she said. Her voice was firm, authoritative, beautiful. He crawled.

Once he reached center stage, the wood flooring hard under his knees, she placed one shiny leather boot toward him. "Lick," she told him. He licked, tongue fully extended, his face down, ass up in the air.

"This is Michael," the auctioneer began, and Mistress Anna placed her other boot under his chin to lick. He licked.

"Michael is dissatisfied with his present Mistress," the man said. *What*? "He feels she is only pretending at their relationship. And she feels it might be time to sell him to someone with more serious intentions." Mike wanted to rise up to his knees and protest, explain that that wasn't true, he was very devoted to his Mistress. But he kept licking the boot.

"Michael is loyal, devoted and obedient. Loves to give service. He has never sucked a cock, but has told his Mistress he gladly would if she ordered him to."

Oh good god, she told them *that*? His face could turn no deeper red. He'd never wanted to be with a man, ever in his life. But the thought of being *made* to do it, for her, well...

Mistress Anna pulled up on his collar, and he rose to his knees, only to find a dildo being pushed into his mouth. There was laughter from the crowd. The dildo was huge, and he had to open his jaws wide to accommodate its sour taste of silicone.

She pulled on his collar and he stood naked in front of at least seventy-seven people, two cocks pointed at them. He could now see heads, people seated around tables, glasses tilting toward lips. Anna made game-show-prize gestures up and down his body, then turned him around.

She pulled him downward, bending him over. "Spread 'em," she said, and he obeyed. He always obeyed.

She pushed his head to the floor and he stood bent over, legs fully spread, ass to the audience.

"Yes, it's virgin, ladies and gentlemen," the auctioneer said as Anna rubbed his smooth cheeks, stroked up and down between them. She patted the back of his balls. "Well, virgin to men. Toys, not so much. Shall we start at ten thousand dollars?"

I can always get up and leave, I can always get up and leave, he thought. This *is* just pretend. A social construct, an agreement. He looked out at the crowd with his head upside down. He couldn't tell if the men or the women were more interested, or repulsed, by his bent-over male ass. What if a man bought him? He shut his eyes.

She turned him around, then pushed him down onto his hands and knees, facing his audience. He waited, until he felt a dab of wet lube against his asshole. *No.*

"This is real," Mistress Anna whispered as she knelt down behind him and fastened a strap-on phallus around her waist. "Keep your head up, and don't you dare close your eyes." He nodded his head, the dildo bobbing with him.

Mike had no idea how much he'd been sold for, let alone who'd bought him. He could only recall a vague jabbering of numbers and a deep sense of shame as he'd held still and kept his eyes focused on the far wall of the ballroom—he'd also felt an equally strong desire not to displease the forceful woman behind him. He remembered immense relief at hearing the gavel slam and feeling both dildos removed. He remembered the click of the leash as Mistress Anna attached it to his collar.

He was now standing with the other sold slaves, all bound and gagged, locked in the coatroom. They were unable to watch the rest of the show; it was none of their business now. But they could certainly hear it. The goddess was still onstage, screaming, crying, even begging for mercy. Mike could hear the repeated crack of a whip—a long, single-tail whip, the real thing. He had never felt one of those.

For once, he couldn't just walk out of this game. Was this even legal? Mike looked at the women, wondering where he'd be taken for the weekend, and they looked back at him, at his big hard dick.

Mike's ass was sore, inside and out. He'd been spanked, hard. It had been quite a show. The organizers had played to every slave's appeal—the pain slut thrashed, the only male emasculated, publicly buggered by a dominatrix. And the cool and collected homecoming queen out there, well, she wasn't so collected anymore.

He heard applause, and the sound of chairs scooting. The door opened and the coat-check girl, wearing a black latex cocktail dress, leashed him and brought him out into the ballroom. "On your knees," she said.

The crowd was ambling toward the doors, talking and laughing. He looked down, away from their faces. Two pairs of shoes stepped in front of him—familiar shoes. "Kiss your new Mistress's feet," the girl in latex said, and handed Mrs. Miller the leash as well as her coat and hat. He bent forward and touched his gag to her relatively expensive shoes, and then Mr. Miller's, as well. Right in front of all these people leaving the ballroom.

"Stand up," Barbara said. Mike stood. He felt his gag being unfastened, and then Carl placed a raincoat over his shoulders, his hands still cuffed behind his back.

Barbara—Mrs. Miller? Mistress?—brought the lapels of the coat together and tightened the belt around his waist. "Put on these loafers," she said, and he slipped his feet into the pair of old leather shoes that Carl dropped onto the floor. "Let's go." She pulled on his leash.

It was dark and raining outside. Mike started to walk toward the limo waiting in the valet queue. He was finally going to be hauled off to a big mansion, to be used as he was in his fantasies, just like in all those novels.

"Where do you think you're going?" Barbara said, tugging on his leash as the rain rolled off her elegant hat. "We're walking. We live two blocks from here."

In a downtown loft? Mike thought. "Yes, Ma'am."

"You will call me 'Mistress,' and Carl 'Master,'" she said. It felt absolutely surreal to be led down a fairly busy urban street, naked and bound under a raincoat, bare legged like some old-fashioned cartoon flasher.

"Yes, Mistress. I'm sorry, my Mistress taught me to call everyone but her 'Ma'am.'"

Barbara stopped and turned, letting Mike stand in the rain as a fedora'd Carl walked on before stopping as well.

"You don't understand, do you?"

Mike shook his head no; he truly didn't.

"We bought you. In perpetuity. Your Mistress has sold you off. You're ours." She started walking, and he was compelled to follow.

If this were for real, Mike would say nothing, accept his fate and follow without question. But this was all a game, an agreement, for crying out loud.

"Mistress?"

"You'll be punished for speaking out of turn."

"Yes, Mistress, forgive me. But I've got to be at work in—"

"How much do you make a year, pouring coffee?"

"What? Oh, uh, twenty thousand?" This really wasn't her business, but what the hell, after tonight.

"We paid three times that for you. Your Mistress sold you because she just doesn't want the same things you do—or that we do. And because she found out she could make the commission, a little finder's fee. Times are tough, you know."

"Yes, Mistress. But I'm—"

"You really haven't been trained very well, interrupting me twice. That'll change."

Mike shut his mouth.

"We found out where you live. Tiny apartment down on Tenth? Not exactly the high life. You'll move in with us. You'll quit your crappy job. You will obey our every command, both of us, twenty-four hours a day, seven days a week. You'll never wear a stitch of clothing."

Mike followed in the rain, barely able to process what he was being told. Of course he could *still* always walk away.

But he wouldn't.

"We live in a big warehouse loft with brick walls and steel beams in the ceiling," she said. "All the better to fasten you to, suspend you from. We throw parties. You'll serve."

Mike swallowed hard, and his stomach began to tighten with the thrill of *possibility*, of not knowing what was next.

"It's not exactly a castle," his new Mistress said, "but it'll have to do."

MELT

Elizabeth Coldwell

It's the most devilishly frustrating thing he's ever done to me. I could almost applaud him for his ingenuity, if only my hands weren't cuffed in place.

The position I'm in is comfortable—to a point. Bryan took the time to ensure I could hold it for as long as is needed. Neither of us knows quite how long that will be, which is the object of this particular exercise. All part of the learning process, as he trains me to be the obedient little submissive he claims he saw lurking beneath the surface the very first time he met me.

I'm standing perfectly still, my movements constrained by my bonds. A translucent plastic collar has been fastened around my neck, and a length of chain passed through the D-ring at its front. Each end of the chain is connected to thick, padded-leather wrist cuffs, and my hands have been arranged so that they are clasped together beneath my bare breasts, in a position of supplication. This also means my forearms offer some support to my tits, keeping the heavy globes thrust upward and out. Bryan has tested my resolve a couple of times by rolling and pinching my nipples, the guitarist's calluses on his big fingers stimulating them in all the best ways until the tender buds are ripe and red as summer berries.

So far, I've held out, but I can't take much more of this stimulation. It sends hot, urgent need pulsing down to my pussy, which has been stuffed with a thick silicone dildo that's held snugly in place by a harness. To complete my ordeal, my legs have been shackled to a spreader bar, but not arranged so far apart that I lose the subtle friction of that big, fake cock inside me. Bryan wants me to be aware at every moment that I am full, plugged to his satisfaction.

In those respects, this is really no different from any other session of bondage training he's put me through. I've learned well, or so I've always thought, absorbing the message that obedience will be rewarded, and gratification will be sweeter the longer it is delayed. I've discovered a place of what I can only call Zen calm in my head, and the longer I stay still and patient, the more a strange, reassuring feeling of well-being permeates my senses. Lost in that secret haven, I can endure all the discomforts of being restrained, punished, frustrated. In the battle of wills between dominant and submissive, it counts as a small victory.

But today he's raised the stakes, finding the perfect way to taunt me with the promise of release.

I thought nothing was out of the ordinary as he fastened me into the collar and cuffs, and slid the well-lubricated dildo up into my pussy—though in truth I'm always wet enough to take that fat length without too much additional help from the moment he orders me to start undressing.

Only once the spreader bar had been secured in place did he reveal his master stroke. He left me for a minute or two while he went into the kitchen. When he returned, he brought with him the ice-cube tray from the freezer. An involuntary shiver went through me at the sight, my mind already imagining how it would feel to have one of those cubes played over my sensitive skin as I writhed in my bonds, helpless to pull away.

What he had in mind for me was something less predictable and far crueler. He popped a wine-bottle-shaped cube out of the tray and brought it over for me to see. Embedded in the ice were two small silver keys—unmistakably those to the cuffs that hold my wrists and ankles in place.

"I thought we'd play a little game today, Kay." My dismayed reaction must have been evident on my face, and Bryan grinned widely in response. "It's called 'let's see how long ice takes to melt.'"

Biting back the groan that threatened to escape from me, I could only watch as he turned the cube this way and that in his fingers, giving me one last lingering look at the keys to my freedom, held suspended in the frozen water. Then he took a double-ended crocodile clip and fed the short length of plastic through one of the loops in my wrist cuffs before clamping each of the toothed clips to the ice cube. This meant that as the ice melted, it would dribble directly into my cleavage, increasing my torment. That's when I realized he really had thought of everything.

"Don't worry, I made sure to turn the thermostat right up. The ice will be gone before you know it. Just think of this as a necessary part of the training."

With that, he dropped a soft kiss on my lips and wandered into the kitchen. The noise of the kettle boiling let me know he was making himself coffee, intent on enjoying his usual Sunday routine of reading the papers with a mug of Blue Mountain in hand.

I don't know how much time has passed since then. He's positioned me so I'm facing away from the clock on the mantelpiece. I can't see how much of the ice has melted; all I'm aware of is the slow, relentless trickle of water down the valley between my breasts and lower, toward my belly. I need it to stop and yet, strangely, I don't want it to end.

For the first few minutes of my ordeal, things were a blur. The sheer deviousness of my master's scheme took my breath away. How long had he been planning all this, and when had he frozen the keys? Or maybe the idea had come to him last night, after I'd gone to bed and left him watching the football highlights. I can just imagine him cracking open a beer and chuckling to himself as he thought about the shock I'd get when he revealed the secret of that ice cube.

I think panic may have set in for the briefest moment. Bryan had never before put me in a position where he couldn't free me the moment things got too much, and I couldn't quite believe he'd done it to me now. Then I took deep breaths, reminding myself that there were duplicates to the keys. He'd have them handy somewhere, and all I'd have to do was call "Red!" and this game would be over.

But I haven't used my safeword in any of our training sessions before, and I don't intend to start today. Now, I am moving toward that place where all is quiet and centered, where the slight burn in my thighs and the strain of keeping in the same position for so long can be ignored. The nagging need to come is another matter. I know that if I keep squeezing my inner muscles around the dildo, I can take myself all the way to the edge, and over it, but Bryan has expressly forbidden me to come without his permission. In other circumstances, I might have disobeyed that command and earned myself whatever punishment was due, but being kept in bondage with that infernal drip of icy water between my tits is already quite enough in the way of punishment, thank you. Not to mention the delicious nipple torment Bryan has returned to administer from time to time.

It might just be my imagination, but I'm sure I can feel the barrel of one of the keys against my skin. Not only is the room pleasantly warm, but the heat of my body is helping the ice to melt faster than it otherwise would. Even so, every minute seems to stretch on forever, time playing the weirdest of tricks on me. I close my eyes and do my best to think about nothing, retreating to my mental oasis of calm and composure.

"How are we doing?" Bryan's voice is soft in my ear. He takes the ice cube between his fingers to examine it. When I look at it, I can see that only the thinnest remnants of ice now surround both keys, and the teeth of the crocodile clips are almost touching. A few more moments, I tell myself, and this will all be over. Though what might happen when the keys are freed and the cuffs removed is another matter entirely.

Bryan's question was addressed to himself. I don't need to reply. He can tell from the flush on my skin and the juices that coat the inside of my thighs just how keyed up I am, how excited obeying him makes me.

"Nearly there now, I think." He lets the cube fall from his grip, and when it lands, it's definitely metal that rests against my skin, not ice. Holding my tit in one big hand, he strums the nipple with his thumb like it's one of his guitar strings.

No longer caring about letting him know how much I need his attention, I moan. Held secure in my bonds, I have happily forfeited all responsibility for my own pleasure. I'm reliant on Bryan, trusting him enough to give me what I need. He knows me so well, and he'll never push me farther than I'm willing to go. It makes him the perfect Master for me, the perfect trainer, and I want to show him how well I'm learning all the lessons he's teaching me.

"You look amazing in bondage, Kay," Bryan murmurs. "And you can't know how hot you make me, with that dildo plugging your pussy. But I bet you want my cock up there, don't you?"

"Oh, Sir, please..." I want that more than anything, but I know I won't get it till I'm free of my restraints. Maybe if I will the keys to fall, I can make it happen by sheer force of concentration.

Bryan plucks at my nipple again. "Maybe I should fuck your ass while your cunt's still full. How would that be, eh?"

I can't form a reply. There's no way I'd be able to take him in my rear hole, not with that big dildo still rammed all the way in me, yet it's such a hot, dirty image it has my pussy convulsing in little spasms around that silicone cock.

That's the moment when the last of the ice melts, and the cuff keys drop to the polished floorboards, landing with an audible clatter. Bryan bends to scoop them up. When he regards me again, his smile is positively feral.

"Looks like time's up. And you've done so well. But there's just one last thing I need to do before you can be released."

My heart sinks. I've waited so long, endured all his torments, and he's still going to keep me restrained? What the hell does he have in mind for me?

Bryan slides his palm between my legs, cupping my pussy. The movement pushes the dildo just a fraction farther in me, and I know it'll only take a little more of this stimulation before my long-denied orgasm hits me.

"Come for me, Kay." It's an order, not a request. "There's a good girl."

He curls his hand up, sliding the chilled keys beneath the webbing of the harness and pressing them to my clit. And I melt.

YOU SHALL NOT COME

D. L. King

"The game is simple. It's your goal to make your partner come and it's your partner's goal not to. We play the first round and then we switch. We keep doing that until one partner comes. We continue to play until the most frigid—I mean the strongest—is left standing. And yes, this is a bondage event."

It was one of those weekend sex camps, the kind where you pay to commune with nature, bugs, heatstroke and poor facilities in order to see friends you seldom get to see and meet other like-minded folks. And, of course, the state-of-the-art dungeons don't hurt—well, you know what I mean. This was only my second time doing the camping thing. I'd kinda hated the first time and sworn I'd never do it again. But Janice talked me into it. She really wanted to go—even after I told her about my previous experience—but she didn't want to go alone.

"Come on, Lydia; it'll be fun. And if you really don't like it, we could move to a motel close by. But it'll be fun," she begged, "you'll see."

I really liked Janice so I figured, what the hell: it's one weekend out of my life—how bad could it be? We were sharing a tent. Yes, I said a tent. At least the bathroom facilities at this place, unlike the other place, were in good condition and the campground employees kept them that way.

The announcer/referee for the game was wearing leather pants and no shirt. It was about a hundred and fifty degrees. Honestly, I have no idea how he was doing it. The saving grace of this particular event was that it had to be played naked. It was Saturday at noon. This was one of the first events and was meant to be a mixer, of sorts—a good way for people to get to know each other, maybe find new play partners. We were in the bondage barn. It wasn't air-conditioned, but there were lights and fans. The announcer continued.

"Okay, if you're playing, move to the center of the barn." People began to move over that way. "Spectators keep back." He walked over to our group and counted heads. There were an uneven number of players. "Hey," he yelled back to the spectators, "anyone else want to play? We need one more person." No one stepped up. "Come on, guys, it's fun. You get to come."

A woman in a G-string and a few beaded necklaces said, "I thought you said the object was *not* to come."

"Yeah, well, it is. But eventually you get to come, right, except for the winner. And, most importantly, you get to play. So, wadda ya say? Anyone want to join us?"

"What does the winner get?" a short guy in the players group piped up.

"I'm glad you brought that up. The winner gets this beautiful trophy." He held up a small, gold sculpture of an icicle. It was pretty cool. "And a twenty-dollar gift certificate good for any item in the vending area."

There was general oohing and ahhing, but no one else stepped up. Finally, one of the guys in our group decided to bow out.

"Come on, Mark, don't leave. It'll be fun," his friend called after him.

"No, you do it, Jeff. I'll just watch. I'll cheer you on."

That left eight of us. The ref ordered us to strip out of whatever we were still wearing and then told us to pair off. One couple, who came together, paired off first. The rest of us found a partner. I got Jeff. We introduced ourselves. Jeff said, "No one has ever made me come if I didn't want to." I told him I loved a challenge.

The referee had each team move to a prepared mat. Each mat had several lengths of rope, several differently sized spreader bars, leather wrist and ankle cuffs, a blindfold, a box of gloves, a medium-sized butt plug, a vibrator, a box of condoms and a bottle of lube. He explained that the top could choose to use any piece of bondage equipment in the barn, or nothing at all. If the top chose to use nothing, the scene would take place on the mat. We could use as little or as much of the equipment as we wanted. The bondage could be as elaborate or as simple as we wanted. There were only two rules; the first was that the bottom's wrists and ankles had to be bound in some way. The second was that there was to be no penetration with anyone's cock. We were free to use fingers and toys, but nothing else. The safeword for the game would be *Red*. Using the safeword would have the same results as reaching orgasm.

"You will be given fifteen minutes to tie your partner and try to make him or her come. When you hear the whistle blow again, you will switch and the bottom will become the top and you will start over. We'll keep switching like that until at least one member of each team has come. Then the winners will form two teams and we will start again until one of each of the remaining partnerships has come.

"The final two will pair off and be given half an hour each. Hopefully, there will be one winner at the end of that time."

Jeff's friend, Mark, piped up from the group of spectators. "But that's not fair. Women can have multiple orgasms. It takes guys longer than fifteen minutes to come again." People turned around and looked at him, some incredulously and some with pity.

"Um, dude, you only get to come once. And then you lose," some guy in the crowd explained.

"Oh, right," Mark said and took a step back.

I looked at Jeff. "Yours?"

"I don't know him. Never saw him before in my life." We both laughed. "You want to bottom or top first?" he asked.

I was pretty sure I could hold out, no matter what he did, but he was cute and I kind of liked him and wanted to watch him in action so I said, "Bottom." That would give me a chance to not only see how he played, but to find out what turned him on, for later.

We picked a mat and the whistle blew. "Lie down on your back," he said. He used a short length of rope to quickly bind my wrists together. He wrapped each wrist separately and then went up and over with a figure eight, making it impossible to escape. Once my wrists were bound, he buckled ankle cuffs on and attached a three-foot spreader bar to them. I immediately closed my knees.

"Think you're smart, huh?" he asked, making a neat triple wrap around each leg, just above my knees. He separated my legs by attaching the two-foot spreader bar to the wraps.

I don't usually bottom and I have to admit, this definitely got my pussy's attention. I could feel the juices begin to gather and my lips begin to puff. My body screamed out to be touched and I rocked my hips against the mat.

"Relax," he said. "I'm not done yet. There'll be plenty of time for that." He doubled a longer length of rope and tied the two loose ends to my ankle cuffs, then pulled the folded end between my wrists. As he pulled, both my legs and my arms came up. Once I was bent like a *U,* he tied the end off and quickly knelt down and put his head between my legs, letting me balance on his shoulders. "So, Lydia," he said, "are you getting a little wet? I think you are. I can smell you," he growled as he ran two fingers up my slit. "Mm-hmm, just as I thought."

He buried them both in my pussy and pumped three times before sliding them out to circle my clit. It felt good. Really good. He sunk them inside me again and leaned forward to lick and suck my nipples. After getting them both wet, he leaned back and blew gently on them, causing them to crinkle and harden. Now, he used his free hand to pinch and pull on them, elongating them, while stroking my interior and using his thumb to circle my clit. I have to admit, it was pretty nice and I think I moaned. But I got distracted when I heard someone scream and then a few people laugh.

"Don't worry about them, Lydia. We have all the time in the world." He curled his fingers up and now his internal stroking was pressing and caressing my G-spot. As my breathing sped up, he kept pace. He removed his thumb from my clit and I groaned. "Oh, you like that, Lydia? Your clit is so swollen. It's absolutely huge," he said. He pressed both fingers against my G-spot and smacked my pussy with his hand, hitting my clit, and I screamed. "Come for me, Lydia. Come for me now," he said, and smacked me again. "Come for me, pretty girl."

I was right on the edge. The guy was good. He raised his hand again and I knew when he smacked me, this time I'd come. Just as he was about to make contact, the whistle blew. He couldn't stop the momentum and as his smack landed, I came in a shower of blue light, my hips rising off the mat.

"Yeah, Jeff! You got her! Way to go, man," I heard his friend yell.

"Ooh, sorry, man," the referee said. "What's your name? Jeff? Yeah, she clearly came *after* the whistle. That doesn't count. You gotta be quicker."

I barked out a laugh and then sighed in my bonds.

It took a few minutes to get everyone free from whatever bondage their partners had devised. I had to admit, simple as it was, Jeff's bondage scene was a good one. I'd been trying to think about what I'd do to him while he was playing with me. It worked, for a while, to keep my mind occupied and off what he was doing, but when my thoughts about playing with his cock mixed with what he was doing to me, it brought me too close to the edge and I had to stop thinking.

The good thing was that he'd been turned on ever since he started to play with me. Currently, his cock was at half-mast, so I knew it wouldn't take much to get him going again. Once the whistle blew, I gathered up some rope and the cuffs, handed him the box of gloves and the medium butt plug, grabbed the lube and condoms and walked him over to a padded, black-Nauga-hyde-covered bondage chair. I seated him with his legs spread, attached the ankle cuffs and clipped them to the rings on the chair legs. I fastened the wrist cuffs and attached his arms to the crossbeam just above his shoulders. His cock jumped when I stood between his legs to bind his arms to the beam with rope.

I smiled and knelt down to gently stroke his shaft. "So you like being bound tightly." I ran my hands over his chest and pinched his nipples lightly. His breath caught. "Mm, yes, such sensitive little buds of skin. Not enough people understand just how sensitive a man's nipples are, do they? It's a shame," I said against his ear. He shivered as I ran the backs of my hands down his chest, making sure to lightly brush the hardened points of his very erect nipples before snapping on a latex glove. The snap caught his attention and he practically salivated while I coated two fingers in lube.

His cock waved and bobbed as I touched his exposed anus with a lubed finger. Oh, he was definitely a fun playmate. I'd like to have lots of time to spend with him. Maybe later, though, as there wasn't much time left to win this game, and I definitely wanted to win. I slowly inserted a slick, gloved finger inside and began to fuck him with it. He couldn't stifle a moan when I inserted a second finger and pumped him harder.

"You like that, do you?" I said, watching his eyes close.

"It's okay," he managed to get out. He was trying to sound unmoved but failing miserably.

"Oh, well then, if you don't want it..." I pulled both fingers out.

"No," he said, before catching himself.

"Mm, I thought so." I pulled the glove off and put a condom over the butt plug. I put another glove on and held the plug up to his face while I coated it in lube. "Shiny," I said, and winked. I quickly inserted it in his already slick hole and pulled off the new glove. "I don't want you to get too complacent," I said as I reached up and pinched both of his nipples. He shrieked but his cock bobbed again. I still hadn't touched it, but I could see it straining. It was a very nice cock. Not too long to be uncomfortable, but long enough to do the job, and a nice width. I could already feel it inside me, feel it filling me...best not to get distracted. The time had to be getting short.

I wrapped my thumb and index finger around the base of his balls and pulled down. "Don't you dare let that plug fall out," I growled in his ear. I smacked first one nipple, and then the other. Hard. He shrieked again but the precome was flowing in a steady stream. I smiled at him and pulled down harder on his balls, keeping them tight below my encircled fingers, keeping the pressure on. His knees started to pull in as I took his cock into my mouth. I circled the head with my tongue, then ground the tip into his frenulum, continuing to tease the sensitive spot with the tip of my tongue.

With a hand on the base of the plug keeping it pushed in tight and rocking it, I swallowed his cock and pumped him a few times before dragging my teeth lightly up his length and circling him just under the rim. I could feel the spasm begin and I released him with a pop just as the first spurt of come flew. I released his balls and watched him come. There were two more good spurts before he was finished, but we still hadn't heard the whistle's blast. As I gently removed the plug from his ass, the referee finally blew the whistle.

I removed the rope binding his arms to the crossbeam and unhooked his wrist cuffs from the eyebolts. He stretched his arms once they were freed and unbuckled the cuffs himself as I unhooked his ankles from the chair. Without being asked, he picked up the used gloves and condom and walked to the trash bin to dispose of them, leather cuffs still buckled to his ankles. He looked really good that way.

We walked back to our mat and I knelt down to unbuckle the cuffs, though I was pretty sure he would have liked to keep them on. "It was the teeth, wasn't it?" I said, looking him in the eye. He shuddered but smiled. "Yes, I thought so."

Someone in each group had come and so we were down to four, or two groups of two. But by that time, I really wasn't all that interested in the game. I was paired with a woman in the next round and I came easily, thinking about what I wanted to do to Jeff. It was all for the best because I didn't want to waste any more time. The game had been a great mixer—exactly what I needed, in fact.

I put on my shorts and T-shirt. Jeff was dressed by that time, too. He'd waited for me. "I thought you'd be going for the gold," he said, "but you lost."

"Did I?" I said. I put my arm around his waist. "Let's get something to eat; that much work makes me hungry." I'd have to remember to thank Janice for dragging me here.

POINT AND CLICK

L. C. Spoering

Nights are long. I enjoy them, and always feel the rush to remind people of that: I like my life, my work. But they are long, and work is work.

I dress carefully every evening: stockings, push-up bra and hair in a bun. I've been doing this for years, and the practice has paid off: I know what they like, and what words to say, motions to make. It's a bit like a play, I think, rehearsed and staged, and when I told a passing stranger I was a performer, I didn't think I was lying. I still don't.

I apply makeup. I don't wear much when I'm out during the day—mascara, maybe, blush and lip gloss—but at night, I get out the eyeliner and palette of eye shadows, the brushes that feel like silk whispers over my skin, the tube of red lipstick that goes on almost obscenely, hanging thick and lush, constantly reminding me of its presence.

My office is three feet from my bed, and I draw a curtain between them, section off one life from another. No one seems to notice the confines of my workspace, the sparse, stark color that surrounds me. I am bright red and pale white and shining brown, clad in black or gray, shedding myself, piece by piece. I learned to talk against the mic of the headset like it's a natural extension long ago; I don't even think about it. What was once an alien creature on my head is part of my costume: my antenna, bug woman, fantasy creature with appropriate accessories, dividing me from the norm. I am set aside, and it shows.

I've been a cam girl, of sorts, since my second semester of college. It was one of those things: you're young, and you're broke, and no one wants to train another waitress who will be gone by the next year, hire on a kid who's never worked a cash register. I had a computer; I had a webcam. The initial investment was an online handle. I had nothing to lose.

Four years later, I can still remember the adrenaline, the fear that coursed through my veins with the first call, the first time I unbuttoned the unremarkable blouse I was wearing for the eager face that shone out from the cam somewhere else in the country. I used what I had, then, clothes I'd collected from thrift stores in high school: knee-high boots and filmy blouses, pencil skirts I hemmed with duct tape and ingenuity. I bought bras on sale, a size too small, so my cleavage swelled up under my chin. The other me was born.

At eight, I open up the store: a few simple clicks, a swipe of my mouse. I leave my laptop on my dresser, next to the overflowing box of costume jewelry, and figurines of horses left over from a ridiculous childhood collection. I never make my bed, but the curtain hides it. This version of me lives on a different plane, in a different atmosphere. She breathes in against the mic and smiles at her next customer.

They're shy, some of them. The handles usually betray them, with macho names and icons attached. Their faces onscreen are drawn, and a little terrified, and I think of the women on phones that came before me when I meet them, leaning in close to the camera.

"Don't worry," I say, my perfectly plucked eyebrows high, a sweet smile made of my slicked-up lips. "It's just you and me."

I take off my top for the first, and talk him through his jerking off of the cock I don't quite see by the angling of his camera. What surprised me, first, about working in front of the cam was how rarely I really ever fucked myself. I'm enough, being there, just there, and the power trip is in only needing to show up to the game.

Some of them are nonchalant, smug, as if I'm the one who clicked through to the chat. I bite my lip and play along. I'm shy for them, hesitant, drawing back layers to pinch at my nipples through my bra, shifting in my seat as though I can't quite resist their charms. Sometimes it's true. It's those clients that confuse me the most.

There was one, back in the beginning, a ten-minute chat where he seemed to be clicking something just off to the right side of my face. I was offended, but felt a neediness rise in me I'd never felt before. My desire was to be the one and only thing he wanted, to please him, to draw all of his attention and a smile that could only be mine, that spent, satisfied gaze of someone who has gotten everything he's ever asked for. He got off, in the end, but the result was unsatisfying, with my screen going black; I signed off for the night early, and lay in bed with my vibrator between my legs, trying to recreate the sensation and never quite getting there.

I get off for the third guy, a dildo pressed into my cunt and fingers in my mouth. I've learned how to keep my eyes on his, on the screen, and so he hums his orgasm with me, stuttering his thanks before he logs off. I wipe my hands on a towel I keep under the desk, and redress, regroup.

I pause when I view my queue. My fingers twitch on the mouse, and I find myself looking back and forth across my little space, like I'm fully expecting someone to hop out of the shadows to tell me I'm being punk'd.

I open the chat, and her face pops up on the screen. I can feel my breaths suddenly becoming shallow, as though they're trying, without me, to make my cleavage heave. "You're back," I say, and the fluttery excitement in my voice isn't feigned.

"Miss me?" she replies, and I can see her cross her long legs, leaning back in her chair.

I don't know why she visits. She's beautiful, and the sliver of her apartment I can see behind her is too well appointed, lavishly decorated. Honestly, she looks too good to be clicking on video chats late on a Friday night. I shouldn't judge—I try not to—but there it is. I expect a certain kind of person to appear on my screen, especially on weekends, and she is not that. She never has been.

I first met her two years ago. Two years in, I was past my clumsiness on the cam, more easily adaptable to situations and surprises. Still, she surprised me: I don't get many women, and, really, she is possibly the most attractive I've ever seen. There's something familiar about her face, and it clicked, one day, that she could be the identical twin to an actress I like, from movies where the girl rides off into the sunset after deeming herself over the guy.

Her handle is innocuous—sbh1199—and, of course, I don't know her name. They tell me sometimes, but she never has. One night, she told me to call her Mistress and I, in a daze I can never replicate with anyone else, did so without hesitation.

"I want you to take your shirt off." Her words snap me back to reality, and I nod, almost too eager, my head loose on my neck and tipping back and forth madly like a bobble head stuck to a dashboard of a car traveling a rough road. I realize I look silly, and feel a blush inch up my neck to my cheeks. My fingers almost fumble on the buttons on my blouse.

"Have you come tonight?" Her tone is conversational, but I still pause, for just a second. No one else asks me about the others: it's not a rule, but it's unspoken, this notion that I'm a stranger who services people this way. She doesn't sound annoyed, or like she's baiting, and, after a moment, I nod, pulling my eyes up to her face there on the screen, biting at the tip of my tongue.

"How many times?" she presses, and she shakes the bracelets decorating her arm down to her wrist, then props her hands on her knee. She is gorgeous, and composed like a photograph.

"Just once," I say, more relieved than I probably should be.

She pauses for a moment, and turns her bracelets with the knob of her knee, covered in the fine, thin fabric of her tights, black and mottled through the grain of the camera's eye.

"How long have you been on tonight?" she asks, and I have a momentary flash to a table in a café, two cups of coffee between us. I know, without a doubt, should she ask me out on a date, I wouldn't hesitate but, as it is, I've never checked where she is. Safety dictates these things, and a form of legality, but I know I would blurt my home address if she so much as asked.

"Just an hour and a half," I say, letting my gaze stray to the clock in the corner of the screen, just for a second. But, in that second, she is standing, and all I can see is the sweep of her skirt and her narrow waistline. I catch my breath.

"Sit tight, little one," comes her disembodied voice, as if she were standing above me, and I do, fingers knotted in my lap and shoulders tense.

She arrives back in front of the camera a couple of minutes later. There is a cost for this absence, but the spread of her house, open to my eyes while she is away from the computer, shows it's expansive, with large windows. She has money. She has that face, and that voice, and that body. Why does she need me?

Settling herself in the chair, she holds up her hand; I squint and lean into the screen, the dim light of her picture making it difficult for me to discern what is wrapped up by her fingers, held up next to her smirk.

She lets me examine, and I swallow when I figure it out, making my headset bob with the motion of my jaw.

"I thought you might like it," she coos, stroking the shaft of the dildo with a manicured hand. "I thought of you when I saw it."

My heart skips a beat, two. Could I have a heart attack right here? Is that possible?

"Me?" I sound mousy to my own ears, and I bite viciously at the inside of my lip in punishment.

"Of course, kitten," she says, and the way she speaks that word sounds like a purr, like she might drag her tongue along the length of my spine and along my neck to flick behind my ear. My skin burns just from the thought.

"I think of you often," she goes on, and crosses her legs, one knee over the other, so that I can see her gently prying her shoe from her foot to place it on the floor. She switches legs, does it again, and then she slides her skirt up her thighs to unclip her garters, beginning the long roll of her stockings, one at a time, down the length of her legs and off the toes of her feet.

"Do you think about me?" she asks, and I have become so hypnotized by her motions, her undressing, that I jump with the question, startled out of my own reverie.

She looks amused, but she waits, her stockings arranged in one hand, the dildo placed obscenely over her lap.

"All the time," I blurt, finally, my tongue sticking to the

roof of my mouth. I'm dizzy, and wonder if she can see it, if my eyes are glassy, if I'm wavering in my seat as much as I feel I might be.

"Good." Her stockings are set aside and now I can see her legs, long and smooth—her knees are bony, and seem a little more swollen than the rest of her legs, but the flaw only adds something to her appearance, making me feel like I'm going to swoon, the heroine of a Victorian novel.

She stands, the dildo resting at attention on the arm of the chair. Her hands go behind her back and I suck in an audible breath; I even hear her chuckle over the headset. "Good things come to those who wait, kitten." It's the second time she's called me that, and I feel something buzz in my chest, a hive of bees woken up in the most unlikely of places.

Her skirt dislodges from her hips and she wiggles out of it, lifting one leg and then the other, a little unsteadily, to take it off. She is not wearing panties. I think I might faint.

"I'd like to see you on your knees, kitten," she announces, face back in frame. I stare at her, and then quickly look side to side at my small office corner; the sheet I use to separate it from my bedroom nearly brushes the back of my chair when I push it back. I have no real room to maneuver.

She waits, though, waits with her blouse nearly open to her black-lace bra and the dildo in her hands. She has a fluff of pubic hair on the slight curve of her mons—black as the hair on her head. I focus on that as I reach behind me to push the curtain along the wire, the rings clicking against each other as they move.

My room behind me can't really be seen, as the lights are off, but I'm acutely aware of how physically I just opened the divide. My mouth feels dry as sand as I push the chair back to find my way to the floor.

"Adjust the camera," she reminds me, and I reach up, angle it down. She nods when she's satisfied, and I find myself already panting, shoulders trembling a little, the nub of the carpet digging into my knees.

"Hands on your desk," she says next, and I lift them there, shoving the mouse and keyboard out of the way so I can lay each palm flat on the surface. My nails are painted, another detail I've become meticulous about, and, for a moment, that's what fills my vision: my cold hands, the purple-painted nails.

"Good girl," she says, almost offhandedly, but I gasp, and then blush at my own reaction, clenching my cunt tight under my skirt.

She smiles and settles back in her chair. I can see her nipples through her bra, now that her blouse has parted and settled under her arms; I can see the rolls her belly forms as she finds a more comfortable position, her legs parted. Even with the grain of the camera, I can see her cunt, wet and swollen. I can't help myself: I lick my lips.

"You like that, don't you?" she hums, and I nod without thinking, already leaning forward in anticipation of her pushing the dildo inside her, all but drumming my fingers on the desk in impatience.

She notices my stance, and stops short. Her legs remain parted, but she stares me down, though it takes me a minute to realize what she's doing and meet her eyes through the computer screen.

"Do you want to watch me, kitten?" she asks, and there is an edge to her voice that was not there before, bringing me up short.

I give a hesitant nod, then nod a bit more firmly. I can hear my heart drumming in my ears so loudly, I almost wonder if she can hear it too.

"You have to learn to be patient," she informs me. The dildo rests against her thigh almost obscenely, and I can practically feel the weight of it against my own thigh, making me squirm in my place.

"I'm sorry," I push out, turning the edges of my lips up in an apologetic smile. "I just...really want to see."

Her face softens, and I let out the breath I didn't know I was holding.

"I know you do, kitten. That's why you're going to have to do as I say."

I nod, again, hard enough to nearly choke myself with the tuck of my chin, over and over.

"You keep your hands where they are. Like I've tied them down," she says. I flex my fingers in place, imagine the ropes she might wind around my wrists, anchoring them to the desk, wrapped around the legs of the furniture, a knot where I can't see it.

"You stay on your knees, kitten," she goes on, and I'm suddenly aware of them, the bend of the joint and the way the bone presses into the carpet, carpet that seems so soft when padding barefoot across it, but is now much firmer, seemingly rocky under my weight.

"I want you to watch me." Her legs are parted wide, but my eyes go to her face, half-shrouded in the darkness that has fallen over her room. It's night where she is too, and the lamps are offset enough that only the barest pools of light lap at her toes and the tips of her hair.

"I want to watch you," I say, and it's like an admission, a confession, my hands pressed to the hard surface of my desk, my wrists burning with the imagined scrape of rope against tender skin.

"I know you do. You have for a long time, haven't you?" The

dildo is in her hand again, and she lets it rub along the length of her labia, the skin catching against the rubber and tugging along—her cunt moves like a mouth, like lips twitching into a smile just before they are kissed. My tongue feels like liquid against my teeth.

We've gotten off together before; I know her face when she comes. But this is different, and I find myself searching her expression for each twitch of muscle and brush of her hair over her forehead. Her fingers are long and graceful; they guide the rubber cock to her slit, pushing just enough that the labia parts and the head inches inside.

"I've wanted you to watch me," she says, as though the thread of conversation is still strung between us, thin and wavering like it's running full with electricity. She lets out a small moan as the dildo moves farther inside her, and I squirm again, finding my cunt against my calf and pressing down to chase some form of release.

"Keep your hands there, kitten," she says, arching an eyebrow though her mouth is slightly agape and she is panting just a little.

"Y-yes," I agree, nodding again, my pinky cramping all of a sudden, as though it knows it's not supposed to move yet needing that movement for no reason at all but to distract me.

"Yes what?" she presses, and I swallow, almost gulp, my heart ringing in my ears once more.

"Yes, Mistress." The word sounds funny on my tongue, and I shake my head a little, embarrassed.

"That's a good girl," she says, then moans again.

The embarrassment dissipates almost immediately, evaporates like alcohol met by heat. I find myself leaning in, getting close enough to the screen that the image blurs slightly, taking her with it.

"Do you know why I call you?" she asks. I'm amazed at her ability to talk: she's pumping the dildo with a slow but steady rhythm, and she's wet enough that it must almost be squirming in her hand, alive.

"No," I reply honestly; I've never understood it. There are a few clients like her, who seem to me to be interesting, attractive people who could likely find any girl to strip and fuck in front of them. This woman, though, shocks me even more.

"I like you," she says, but with a slight lingering over the last word, so that I know she is going to keep talking. "You're quite different, you know."

I watch her hand clutching the dildo; she has pushed it fully inside of her, and is drawing it out at a leisurely pace. It is slick with her juices.

"I am?" I ask finally, biting at my lip, though I do remember she told me not to—it's a habit, a nervous one. My heart is beating so hard, I'm sure my skin is quivering over it on my chest, at my pulse points, making me vibrate on the cam.

"Look at yourself. Tell me you aren't." She is fucking herself harder now, just a little, and a little grunt emits from her nose with each deep plunge of the dildo. I am wet under my skirt, my own cunt throbbing with need.

I know instinctively not to disagree, but, moreover, I realize she is right: if she is paying attention to me, there is something special. Not only that, it's indicative of something larger than her, larger than me.

I moan, leaning closer to the desk, my fingers pressing hard but my wrists still where she assigned them, my imaginary bonds keeping me in place. I wish they were actually there, wish the harsh rub of the fibers was what kept me in place outside this sudden burst of heavy, needy obedience.

Her moan catches the end of mine, as if we share a brain,

body, voice. My eyes pop open with the desire to see all of her, to not miss a second. The dildo is now slick, her cunt full and purple, and I can see her knees trembling ever so slightly. I want to fuck myself, but the only relief I have is baring down, rather futilely, on the side my calf, where only the slight pressure gives me any sensation at all. I can feel my own cunt pulsing, grasping at the nothing in the air, and whine just as she all but explodes, her ass rising up off the chair with her orgasm, her hand still working the dildo hard and deep inside her.

Her cunt shines, and I lick my lips, imagining the taste of her on my tongue. Her face contorts with the sensations, and then irons out, sweet, like she might fall asleep right there with her body exposed to me and the camera, as if she is perfectly safe before me. She is—of course she is.

"You'd clean me up, if you were here," she says after the silence, punctuated only by both our rapid breaths, has gone on long enough.

"Y-yes, Mistress." I still fumble over the word, even as it feels more natural on my tongue. I want to whisper it in her ear, I want to sit at her feet and purr like a kitten with her fingers in my hair. I don't notice the hard floor under my knees anymore; I am absorbed in the electricity that is flowing through me, the dampness of the skirt between my legs, and her gaze upon me.

"I like you there," she goes on, setting the wet dildo aside. "I like you watching; I like that you want it but can't have it. Do you like it too?"

I nod before I've even formed the thought in my mind, but know she is right. She is plucking the knowledge right from my brain, with only the way her eyes stare through the camera and into me.

"I'll call again, kitten," she says. "Next time, I want you to start on your knees."

I open my mouth, but the screen goes black. Now the only sound is my heart slamming in my ears, my breath coming in gasps out of my slack-jawed mouth.

Unsteadily, I get to my feet, shut down the program. Some nights, I work well into the morning. Tonight, it is not even midnight. I stand before the computer, in the confines of my little space, and rub my wrists, which feel bruised. I stare at them, wishing the purple to the skin, yet only able to imagine the coarse sensation of rope rubbing a path, endless circles, keeping me in place.

STUCK ON YOU

Jenne Davis

Jane watched in silence as Mike moved across the room. She loved to watch him move, his strong and powerful arms now braced and all muscle as he hauled the steaming bucket of hot water toward her.

"Do we have everything now?" he asked. His voice had a certain authority that she'd always been attracted to.

"I think so," she replied, looking down at the tools that seemed to have spilled across the entire length of the room. "It feels like we brought most of the store, to be honest."

"Yes, yes it does," Mike replied, glancing at the myriad of toys that filled the room. "I think we're all set, hon. Ready, steady, go..."

Jane picked up the wallpaper scraper and got to work at his command, but a part of her felt guilty as she began to score the old paper that surrounded and encased what was once her parents' bedroom. So many good memories had been made in this room, but they'd been marred by the last one: the passing of her father. She had lain next to him as he'd slowly sunken into a coma from which he would never return.

Her father had given her permission to do with the house and this room as she saw fit. She knew that the time was right to erase not only the decor that was so familiar to her, but also that sad memory. She was ready to move on, and as she looked at Mike, she began to scrape a little more furiously.

Mike had been there through the worst days and the best nights. He'd made her feel a little better as the light had dimmed from her father's eyes each day, held her in this very room when he passed, and now he was helping her create new memories.

"You okay, babe?" The concern was evident in his voice as well as his eyes when she glanced his way.

"Yeah, I'm fine...just, well, you know..." She wanted to finish but somehow couldn't find the words.

"I know this isn't easy, but I'm sure it's what he would have wanted."

"Me too," was all she could manage before the floodgates opened up and the tears came forth.

"Oh, babe, it will be okay." Before she could think of anything to say, he was holding her in his arms. She took strength from those arms, the arms that had held her after the funeral, the arms that had captured so many of her tears over the years, the arms that she relied upon.

"I know, I'm okay. I promise." She looked up at him and found his lips rushing to meet hers. It was a kiss she didn't want to stop, a kiss she could get lost in, and yet she knew that there was work to do so she pulled away from him.

"Let's get this done, shall we?"

"Yes, let's! This is gonna take a lot of hard work but it will be worth it in the end, I promise." He released her from his comforting grip, and stood beside her, his own scraper raised and ready to go to work.

Once more she took her scraper and began to score the paper. This time, she felt a new sense of achievement with each small piece of wallpaper that left the death grip of the wall.

"Boy, what did they put this stuff up with?" Mike asked.

"Something very, very sticky," she replied with a giggle. This was proving to be much harder work than either of them had envisioned at the beginning of the day. Jane stopped for a second and reached into the bucket for the large sponge and began to apply it to the two-by-two piece of wallpaper she'd just scored. Despite the fact that they had been on the job since eight, all they'd achieved was stripping about one half of a side of the room. Even that had more than a few spots of the old floral wallpaper remaining. "It's sure not as easy as they made out in the store," she mused, giving him a sideways glance. "Coffee?"

"Sounds like a plan to me. I'll put the kettle on." He dropped his scraper on the floor and proceeded to the kitchen.

Jane stood back and admired their work, pleased they were making progress but at the same time annoyed that they hadn't gotten more done. She turned her back on the bare piece of wall and sighed upon looking at the pieces that remained. As she made to move toward the door, Jane found herself falling backward against the bare but very sticky piece of wall they'd been working on. She tried to right herself but couldn't. The sticky residue held her in place.

"Mike? Mike? I could use a hand here," she called as it became apparent to her that getting out of this mess wasn't something she could accomplish alone. Each time she tried to pull away the glue seemed to hold her tighter, tugging painfully at her skin.

Mike ambled back into the room, his eyes widening at the

scene that greeted him. His wife was all but spread-eagled in front of him. His eyes instinctively traveled down her body before taking in the camel toe that had formed between her legs. Her bare breasts—she didn't wear a bra for this kind of work—were fighting against the fabric that was apparently as stuck to the wall as she was. He began to chuckle, but caught himself as he noticed the fear in her eyes.

"You think this is funny?" Jane asked, but even as she did, a small part of her appreciated the way he'd just looked at her—almost like he was glad she was stuck, at his mercy.

"What the hell? How did you manage that? Try moving."

"What do you think I've been trying to do?" A slight tinge of desperation rang out in her voice.

"Okay, let's try this." Mike took her arm and carefully tried to remove it from the sticky mess.

"Ouch, that hurts."

"Sorry, baby, you know I'd never hurt you, but we have to do something."

He stood back and looked deep in thought for a moment, before reaching forward and plucking the large soapy sponge from the bucket. Gently, he began to apply it behind her right hand.

His closeness warmed her once more, and a familiar sensation began to build between her inner thighs. His nearness made her warm once again, the sensation building up from between her legs. Slowly, the gummy paste that held her began to give way, but she was starting to think maybe she didn't want it to, at least not yet.

"This is gonna take a while," he announced as he dipped the sponge once more into the bucket.

She felt so vulnerable as Mike moved across her body applying the soap, slowly peeling her from her prison, yet that same vulnerability was strangely sexy. With each stroke of the soapy water, each time she managed to peel herself a little freer, her inner thighs began to moisten. With him so close, she wanted nothing more than to touch him too, but she was afraid to move in case she got stuck once more. Being immobilized, even under these circumstances, was in fact turning her on more than she would care to admit.

She could smell his familiar aroma as he reached forward and kissed her gently. "You're doing fine. We'll have you out of here in no time." The words reassured her, as did his gentle kisses, but suddenly she wanted more. She couldn't explain it to herself and she couldn't say it out loud. Instead, she showed him, her tongue reaching into his mouth and almost devouring him. He'd always been able to read her before and this time was no exception; there was no mistaking what she wanted him to do. He took his cue, meeting her lips with the same ferocious fervor.

Still grasping the waterlogged sponge, his hands began to travel across her body, this time with an altogether different purpose. His breath came fiercely, filling her ears as he used the sponge to leave a sloppy, soapy mess on her breasts, her nipples hardening at the exposure to the now slightly cold substance. Giving her a sly smile, he reached between her legs with his free hand, his smile widening as he felt the wetness that definitely wasn't caused by the water running down from her T-shirt.

Feeling exposed like this, waiting for Mike to free her—or not—and knowing she could do nothing about it, turned Jane on to the point where reason left her. She all but screamed as his wet hand reached her inner thighs. She couldn't move away from the wall, but she didn't want to. Once more he kissed her deeply, signaling his own need for some kind of release. Before she could utter the words that were on the tip of her tongue he pulled away from her. He had tugged, pulled and torn the skimpy fabric of her shorts away from her body, leaving her stuck and exposed, but oh so turned on. He turned his attention to her already ruined T-shirt and ripped it in two with one pull.

Her breasts spilled forward, no longer held by the formfitting material. When the cool air hit them, she caught her breath. Mike stood back, admiring his handiwork for just a moment. All thoughts of getting free had left her brain, instead replaced by pure lust. She could see his desire in his eyes, as he wielded the sponge once again, as if it were a unique toy.

"You look like a masterpiece." His eyes were smiling as the words left his mouth, before he began to strip off his own clothes. His rugged chest, powerful thighs and glorious dick came into view, making her hunger for him even more. Now all she wanted to do was reach forward and touch him. Instead she just stayed stuck in the same position, spread-eagled against the wall, waiting for his touch, to feel his naked skin against hers. She knew resistance to the sticky glue was futile, but still her body tingled, her nipples hardening and mouth watering at being so close, yet so far, from the only man who could make her feel this way. Thankfully, she didn't have to wait long.

In mere moments, cool water ran from the sponge down the length of her body. His hard dick brushed against her leg, causing her to sigh. The water ran in rivulets between their hot and sweaty bodies. He ground against her, pushing her deeper into the wall, holding her tighter than any glue ever could. Would he take her right there, leave her pinned, captive between his hardness and the wall? Did she want him to? Jane moaned at this delicious dilemma, trying to shift her body to ease him inside her.

Then, without warning, Jane found herself free as the glue let go all at once. The soapy water had done its trick. They both tumbled forward onto the carpeted floor. Jane found herself underneath a hot, soapy and very horny Mike, grateful to once again be sandwiched between her true love and a hard surface, unable to escape. In their brief encounter, she'd come to appreciate the thrill of being stuck, caught, captured.

In what seemed like seconds he was inside her. For so long she had been wrapped up in this room, stuck on its contents and all the bad memories that it contained. Now, as he filled her very existence, she forgot the pain and anguish of the past few months. They washed away as easily as the old glue that had bound her to the wall. With so much buildup, her body was more than ready for him, primed for a release of the most powerful kind. As the orgasm washed over her, she wrapped her arms around his and let go, embracing freedom in more ways than one. Mike moaned as he looked down at her, maintaining the connection that had sparked this impromptu coupling as his wet, slippery body ground against hers. The look in his eyes made her feel as she had when she'd been stuck to the wall—he would take care of her, no matter what. When she felt him climax inside her, her own pleasure rose again, joining his.

As they both came down from their respective orgasms, she looked into his eyes, giggled and said, "I've always been stuck on you, but never like that. Don't put the sponge away. I think we're going to need it again. We've got a whole room to finish."

IN SUSPENSE

Shenoa Carroll-Bradd

Before they began, all was silent. Christie and Mac entered the stain-proof room together, fingers entwined in solidarity.

Christie's stomach tightened, and her skin flushed and tingled, just as it had when she'd first met Mac almost a year ago. She wanted this, and there was no way she'd let nerves stand in her way.

Mac closed the door behind them before leaning in to kiss the spiral of rings up her earlobe, his breath teasing and warm.

Her nipples hardened as his kisses sent tingles up her scalp and down her spine. Christie leaned back against Mac and tilted her chin up, giving him better access to her neck and raising her gaze to the chains hanging from the ceiling like glowworm strands with bright steel hooks at their ends. She could do this, damn it.

Everything Christie loved had come hand in hand with pain, whether it was her Akita, Ponzy, who had only been adopted because her previous dog ran off, or the dozen tattoos adorning her skin. Those carefully inked designs had taken hours in the chair. This would only take minutes.

Mac wrapped his arms around her waist. "Hey," he said between kisses. "It's okay. We'll start off slow."

Christie raised a hand to fondle his zero-gauge earlobe before leaning in for a kiss. His lips parted, and she darted her tongue inside, playing with his silver stud.

He kissed back, harder, sliding one hand down to cup her ass and pull her against him.

She ground against his pelvis, feeling an erection swelling behind his jeans.

"Tell me when you're ready."

Christie nodded, moaning against his mouth, but did not answer. Not yet. She pulled back to peel his shirt up over tight abs and past his pierced nipples, exposing his chest piece: the MacMillan family crest bordered with thistles and bookended by a pair of intricately detailed raven's wings. She ran her hand down it just once, though she'd seen it almost every day for months now. Still, the familiar design made her smile. Christie thought of it as a link between Mac and his ancestors, tracing ink back through the years to his distant highland predecessors, whose fiery coloring he still wore in a stripe down his scalp, and on the end of his chin.

He grinned, mischievous as ever, and tugged at the buttons on her blouse, pulling it open, letting air in over her flushed skin. Mac slipped a hand inside, massaging her right breast while he worked on the other buttons.

She kissed him in little bursts, darting in to press her lips to his, then pulling back before he had a chance to respond, teasing him into trying to follow when she retreated.

Mac slipped the last button free and her shirt slid down her arms, dropping to the floor. He cupped her face and pulled her into the deep kiss she'd been withholding.

Christie laughed against his lips, reaching down to unbutton her jean shorts. She hadn't put on underwear that morning, a decision she hoped she wouldn't regret later, once she was exhausted and sore. The denim was already damp from her growing excitement.

Mac hooked a finger into the waistband, helping to tug them down. When the denim hit the floor, Christie stood naked before him, wearing just her tattoos. They helped her feel brave, like little flags proclaiming, *I'm no stranger to pain. I have no fear of it. I take it in, and the pain makes me more beautiful.*

They stood together, her face cradled in his hand, just breathing. Mac's muddy green-brown eyes held hers, and after a moment he asked, "Are you sure you're ready for this?"

Christie pressed her lips together and nodded. "Absolutely. I've always wanted to try suspension, but it never felt quite right with anyone else. It requires a specific kind of trust." She leaned forward to playfully run her tongue across his lower lip. "A trust I've only felt with you."

Mac kissed her, smoothing a hand down her flat stomach, curling two fingers up to stroke between her slick lips until she rocked back and forth to his rhythm.

She knew what he was doing—taking her mind off of it all, flooding her system with endorphins—and she appreciated it. After a moment of bliss, Mac pulled away from the kiss and stepped over to the door, rapping thrice against it before rejoining her. He kissed her again, cradling her naked shoulders against his chest as the door behind them opened, and two tattooed men entered wearing surgical masks and gloves.

"We're ready," she said, stepping out of Mac's embrace. *If I can do this, I can do anything.*

The attendants' eyes didn't linger on her bare skin, though she felt an electric thrill at their presence. The men very carefully and professionally positioned her beneath the hooks, and began their work.

Christie and Mac had set up their appointment two months in advance, just in case either party had second thoughts, and to be sure all arrangements were in place. She had been weighed, measured and gauged on their last visit a week ago, so the hooks could be perfectly adjusted for her size and frame.

The attendants sat Christie on a stool covered in a disposable plastic sheet.

Mac stood by, offering his hand to squeeze, which she gladly accepted.

The attendant to her left started the suspension, pulling up a sizable piece of skin on the outside of her thigh and pushing one of the bright, clean hooks in until it popped through and slid out the other side.

Christie stared at the hook in her skin, clenching tight to Mac's hand, watching the man slide the shiny curve into position in the freshly pierced hunk of flesh before moving on. She came back to herself after a moment, looking around as if she'd just woken, her whole body tingling with a mix of pain and excitement.

"Doll," Mac leaned in, "are you okay?"

"I..." Christie watched, rapt, as the other attendant did the same, popping the hook through her skin so she was symmetrical again.

"You what?"

Christie looked at him, a slow smile spreading over her face, a tightness spooling in her chest, identical to the winding beginnings of arousal. She bit her lip and fought the urge to grind her naked cunt against the plastic-covered seat. "I thought there'd be more blood, that's all."

The attendant to her left looked up, his warm eyes crinkling into a smile over the mask. "Glad to disappoint."

She squeezed Mac's hand for every hook the attendants placed in her thighs, upper calves and knees, and while there was no denying the piercings hurt, the pain was not what she'd expected. It was far from unbearable, and the sensation of cool metal moving beneath her skin was so deliciously novel, Christie barely noticed the pain with so much discovery blooming inside her.

The attendants worked quickly, their gloved hands deft with practice, but still gentle.

Despite everything else, Christie felt goose bumps break out along her arms, and she bit back a quip about never having had three men's hands on her at once. Mac wasn't really the jealous type, but she felt a new level of bond developing between them in the suspension chamber, and didn't want to tarnish it with a cheap joke.

When the technicians finished inserting the hooks, Mac moved behind her, as discussed, and placed his hands on her shoulders. One attendant moved to the side and began to work the pulleys, drawing her knees up, while the other carefully removed the stool from beneath her. Mac's hands went from resting atop her shoulders to cupping them as her torso moved parallel with the floor, shifting finally to support a fraction of her weight as her head came down to point at the ground.

"Whoa..." she murmured.

"Are you o—"

"I'm fine," she insisted, cutting off the question. He sounded more worried than she felt, and she didn't have any room for doubt just then.

The attendant who had removed the stool pulled back the edge of his glove to inspect his watch. "You have eight minutes in the air, starting now."

Eight minutes. That's nothing. I can do eight minutes with my hands tied behind my back. Blood was already rushing to her head; she could feel it heating her cheeks and pounding a sweet rhythm in her ears. She felt Mac's hands on her inner thighs, pressing them apart. The pressure from the hooks in her skin increased when he took his hands away from her shoulders, and Christie bit back a short gasp. Instead of trying to look up at him, she gazed at the clean white floor, grinning at the strange sight of her short blonde hair hanging down like Spanish moss. She could see the attendants' shoes at the edges of her vision, but Christie didn't care. She was floating, like a fairy. Like an upside-down angel.

Above her, Mac's breath tickled her thighs as he laid a quick succession of kisses down to her left hip bone, then the hands returned to her shoulders, lifting her just a little, taking some of her weight off the hooks.

Christie groaned, not out of pain, but out of need, wanting nothing more than to have him, right there. Her head swam, and she felt dizzy with desire.

Mac lowered his mouth to her aching cunt, sucking her clitoris gently between his teeth and flicking his tongue across the engorged pearl until she gasped and cried aloud, unconcerned with their audience. Working in tandem with his tongue, Mac lifted and lowered her shoulders in time with each lap and thrust, easing her weight on and off the hooks, sending ripples of pain and pleasure coursing through her suspended body.

"Five minutes," the attendant said from the corner. His voice sounded far away, faint and unimportant.

Had three minutes already passed? Her head spun. Christie could hardly catch her breath. Between the pull of the hooks, the blood rushing to her head, and the sweet magic Mac was working between her legs, she felt the most powerful orgasm of her life building in her core and rushing forward on a tidal wave of sensation. Christie's body was wracked with waves of shuddering climax, shaking so fiercely in the clutches of ecstasy that the chains rattled and chimed like sleigh bells, drowned out by her echoing cries of shattering joy.

Christie awoke cradled in Mac's arms, feeling safe and loose and content. He'd wrapped her in a blanket. She rolled her head back onto his collarbone, pressing a kiss to his stubbly ginger jaw. "Why are we on the floor?" she asked sleepily, feeling like a contented cat in a sunbeam.

Mac's arms tightened. "Because you passed out for a minute and scared me half to hell. The technicians brought you down and patched you up." He flicked the blanket aside to show her the sterile gauze squares taped to her right leg. "They think all the blood rushing to your brain, coupled with the orgasm, must have overloaded your circuits." He kissed the top of her head. "Are you—?"

"I'm okay," she finished for him. "I'm more than okay. I'm… amazing." She snuggled deeper into his arms.

"Yes, you really are." Mac squeezed her tighter. "Can you stand? We need to get you home."

With Mac's help, Christie rose on wobbly, tender legs, and got redressed, grateful for her lack of underwear—one less article to pull up over her new bandages. As she buttoned her blouse, Christie gazed at her lover through her eyelashes, shy as a coquettish schoolgirl. "You know what this means, don't you?"

Mac paused, holding up his shirt. His moss-brown eyes widened. "What?"

Christie crossed the three short steps to his side and stretched up to plant a sweet, soft kiss on his mouth. "Now it's your turn."

Mac stared at her for a moment, the corners of his mouth slowly creeping up into the mischievous grin she loved. "Do you dare me?"

"I dare you."

Mac swept her into his patchwork-sleeved arms, holding her close against his chest, her flushed cheek pressed to the MacMillan family crest, as if inviting her to join the legacy.

TRINITY'S NEW HOBBY

Lucy Felthouse

Trinity heard Colton's key in the door, then him calling out. "Hey, Trinity, I'm home!"

"In here," she said, continuing to concentrate on what she was doing, her hands moving methodically, rhythmically.

Footsteps on the wooden floor, then his voice again, closer. "What, not meeting me at the door? Flinging yourself into my arms and welcoming me home, sexy style?"

"I'm not doing anything until I've finished this row," she said without looking up.

Colton tutted. "What are you doing, anyway? Crochet? Did an alien steal you away and replace you with a granny that looks exactly like you?" Moving around the sofa, he dropped down next to her.

"Hey! Watch it! You nearly made me drop a stitch." Clutching extra hard at her needles, she inspected the work carefully to make sure she hadn't, in fact, dropped a stitch.

Sniggering, Colton shot back, "Sorry, granny."

"It's not funny. I've worked bloody hard on this, and there's no way I want to screw it up now. And in answer to your question, no I'm not crocheting. I'm knitting. I've just started recently. And I haven't been a victim of an alien invasion. I just enjoy it, all right? It's relaxing, and unlike your favorite hobby of watching TV, I actually get something out of this at the end."

Colton shrugged. "Whatever. I like to watch TV to relax, you like to knit." He paused. "You've got to admit it's kinda old-fashioned, though."

Trinity reached the end of her row, carefully put the point-protectors on to stop the garment slipping off the needles, then placed the whole thing down on the coffee table. Turning to her boyfriend with a wry expression, she said, "Actually, I'll have you know, knitting's cool again. Crafting in general is experiencing a massive revival. Something to do with the recession, I think. People staying in more, wanting to save money. Making gifts instead of buying them..."

"Okay, okay." He held his hands up. "I get it. Knitting's cool." Pointing at the mass of wool on the table, he asked, "What are you making, anyway?"

"A jumper. For myself, before you panic. I'm not going to start making cutesy things with animals or bobbles on and forcing you to wear them."

Colton huffed out a breath. "Thank god for that. Just 'cos you're a granny all of a sudden, doesn't mean I want to start dressing like a granddad."

Fixing her boyfriend with a look that should, by rights, have turned him to stone, Trinity snatched up her knitting and flounced out of the room. She headed for their bedroom, where she kept her knitting stuff neatly in a corner of her wardrobe. Putting her hard work away carefully in her bag, her fingers brushed against a spare length of cut-off yarn. The thick blue wool gave her an idea. Grinning, she gently pulled it out. Yes, it would do nicely.

Just then, she heard Colton muttering to himself, then his progress from the living room to their bedroom. He was probably coming to apologize. She smirked. Well, she'd make him grovel, all right.

Quickly, she grabbed the chair that leaned up against the wall and shifted it into the large space between the bed and the door, with it facing the bed.

Colton walked in just as she'd stepped back, and his gaze landed on the chair. He frowned, then looked at her. Shaking his head, he adopted a gently smiling expression. "Look, babe, I'm sorry. I didn't mean to upset you. I was just teasing you, which I know doesn't excuse what I said, but I definitely wasn't trying to hurt you. I don't mind what hobbies you have, as long as you're happy." He paused, his smile growing wider, more hopeful. "Forgive me?"

Giving him a cool smile, she pointed at the chair and snapped, "Sit down."

Frowning again, Colton stepped over to the chair and lowered himself into it. "W-what are you doing?"A look of realization crossed his face, and his confusion morphed into pure delight. "Ahh, are you gonna give me a lap dance?"

Trinity resisted the temptation to roll her eyes. "Yeah, babe," she said lightly, much more lightly than she felt. "Something like that. Close your eyes."

Clearly convinced it was his lucky day, Colton did as she ordered, still smirking.

Letting her irritation and frustration show on her face now, Trinity crossed over to the chair and stepped behind it. Swiftly pulling the wool out to its full length, she then set about securing Colton's wrists to the chair. The yarn was super chunky, but she wasn't sure quite how strong it was, so she wrapped it around twice, making sure it wasn't so tight it would cut off his circulation. Examining her handiwork, Trinity was surprised at herself. They'd never fooled around with bondage before, and yet she'd managed to tie Colton up, quickly and safely. Apparently those smutty books she'd been reading were informative as well as erotic.

"Ooh, getting a little kinky are we, sweetie?" Colton asked. He sounded excited rather than worried, which made Trinity's job easier, not to mention much more fun.

"Yes, darling," she purred, standing and moving to his side, leaning down and nibbling his earlobe, eliciting a guttural groan from his throat. "I thought a bit of bondage would be fun. So I've tied you up with wool."

"With *wool?*" Colton's eyes flew open—wide open—and he gazed at his girlfriend. "Seriously?" He fidgeted in the seat, wriggling his arms and trying to twist his neck to see the unusual form of bondage.

"Yep. I thought it would be a good idea to show you that knitting isn't as boring or as granny-ish as you seem to think."

Colton groaned, this time in disappointment and frustration. "So I'm not getting a lap dance. You're going to sit there, knitting, and make me watch, aren't you?"

Shaking her head, Trinity replied, "No. Though I hadn't thought of that. Any more of your cheek and that's exactly what I'll do. In a way, though, what I have planned is worse. Much worse."

He opened his mouth to speak, then seemingly thought better of it, and kept quiet.

With a curt nod, Trinity flashed Colton what she hoped was a seductive grin and began to undress. He remained silent, transfixed, as she tugged off her jumper, then the T-shirt beneath.

Bending slowly, giving Colton a tantalizing view of her breasts hanging heavily in her bra, she removed her socks, then kicked the pile of shed clothes away from her. Next, she spun around, undoing her belt, then the button and zipper of her jeans. She unhurriedly inched them down, now treating him to the vision of her exposed buttocks, bisected by her lacy black thong, and her thighs, too, as the jeans bunched up around her ankles.

Before long, she stepped out of them, shoving them toward the other items she'd removed. Now, with equal speed—or lack of it—she slipped down her panties. Once they were on the pile, leaving her utterly naked, she flashed Colton her wickedest grin, biting her bottom lip.

He strained at his bonds, but it was fruitless—the super-chunky yarn was doing a job, albeit not the one it had been intended for.

Satisfied Colton wasn't going anywhere, Trinity settled back on the bed, still facing him. She was going to give him a show and a half. First, she sucked the index and middle fingers of her right hand into her mouth, getting them good and wet. Slicking the saliva over each of her nipples in turn, she repeated the process, then began to tweak the rapidly hardening buds.

It wasn't long before she felt slickness between her thighs. Because her plan had formed and been carried out so fast, there'd been no anticipation, no time for her body to catch on. But ever since she'd tied Colton up and begun stripping in front of him, her libido had gradually been ramping up. Now, as she plucked at her tits, zings of delicious arousal licked their way along her nerve endings, pooling in her groin. Already her labia were growing fat, and her clit throbbed.

Forcing herself to hold on longer, just a little bit longer, to draw out Colton's agony, she grew rougher with her nipples. Her rolls and squeezes became full-on tugs and pinches, elongating the sensitive flesh and drawing moans and groans from her parted lips.

A glance at her fella told Trinity that she was most definitely having the desired effect, and she hadn't touched her pussy yet, or even shown it to him. She decided it was time for both of those things. Leaning back on her left hand, she parted her legs and slipped her right hand between them.

Colton made a strangled sound as her sex was revealed to him, already wet and swollen, so close but ultimately out of reach. Trinity played around, dipping her fingers just inside her cunt and swiping the juices over her vulva and clit. Again and again she touched and teased, until she couldn't hold back any longer. Her boyfriend's expression, his blatant need for her, were as arousing as her touch, and now her clit ached so much it was almost painful.

Scooping up more of the copious fluid that flowed from her, Trinity stroked it over her clit, jolting slightly at the sensitivity she found there. It wouldn't take much to make her come, that was obvious. Zoning in on the tiny spot near the bundle of nerve endings that really got her going, she rubbed, building up to exactly the pressure and rhythm that got her off. At the same time, she watched Colton watching her, and got a huge kick out of how he reacted to her every move, his eyes wide, jaw slack, his fidgeting and the probably unconscious jerking of his hips.

Splaying her thighs even wider to ensure Colton was getting a really good view, she continued masturbating without holding back, every movement bringing her closer to climax. It wouldn't be long...

Throwing her head back, she picked up her pace, not caring about the discomfort in her right hand. Coming was more important in that instant, and as the tightening in her abdomen increased, the tingles between her legs began; she knew she was on the precipice.

Apparently Colton knew, too. "God, oh god, babe, you look so fucking hot. Please let me fuck you."

Blatantly ignoring him, Trinity let her fingers push her over the edge, an almighty climax crashing into her, making her cunt clench, her juices flow and her throat grow hoarse. It took all of the energy she had to stay relatively upright, as she wanted to watch her boyfriend's reaction as she came right there in front of him, not allowing him to do anything except watch.

Her pleasure held her in its grip of oblivion for several long seconds, but as soon as she broke free enough, she opened her eyes again and looked at him.

Mouth agape, eyes almost popping out of his head and with an erection threatening to burst from his trousers, it seemed he'd definitely enjoyed the show.

"So," she said, snapping her legs shut and fixing him with a stern look, "still think I'm a granny?"

Colton shook his head so fast he probably gave himself neck strain. He looked so eager, so damn horny, that she almost took pity on him.

Almost.

PLASTERED

Anna Watson

Nate stood outside the gym, inhaling the cool evening air. He'd had a great workout in yoga class, with the added perk of getting to observe not only the very fuckable yoga instructor, Patty, but several other hot women in the class. His favorites were Alice and her friend Victoria, and it was Alice he was thinking about now. From the way he'd caught her sneaking peeks at his meat, nicely displayed in his formfitting yoga pants, he was sure she would accept when he asked her out, which he planned to do ASAP. Smiling lecherously as he thought of the sweet view she'd shown him of her luscious tits when they'd done downward-facing dog, Nate turned down the alley that led to his car.

He was ambushed almost immediately. Two women wearing tightly belted raincoats, stiletto heels and garishly colored Mardi Gras masks, were suddenly on either side of him. The blonde jammed something cylindrical into his side—it could have been a lipstick tube or a gun—and they hustled him to the mouth of the alley where a car was idling. The redhead twisted his arm, her long blue nails digging into his flesh. Before he knew exactly what had happened, he was wedged between them in the back-seat while the driver, another woman, gunned the motor and drove expertly though the dark streets.

Clearing his throat, he attempted to speak, but the redhead slapped a hand over his mouth and hissed, "No talking, baggage," so Nate held his tongue.

"And no looking," added the blonde, tugging a black rubber hood over his head and pulling the drawstring tight. Nate, struggling to breathe, thought briefly of calling out, trying to appeal to the driver, attempting to muscle past the women and jump out of the car, but the press of their bodies was beginning to excite him. He might as well play along with them for a little longer. They were only girls, after all. How hard could it be to escape?

The car stopped and Nate allowed himself to be yanked into a building and up a flight of stairs. The women guided him roughly inside, where he was pushed violently onto a hard, narrow surface. Laughing delightedly, the women moved his limbs with firm hands until he was stretched out on his back. They pulled off his hood, revealing harsh fluorescent lights that hurt his eyes. Before he could get his bearings, he felt straps binding his ankles, thighs and chest, anchoring him tightly to what he could now see was some kind of medical examining table. The blonde loomed over him. She had removed the raincoat to reveal a red-latex catsuit with a high neck and long sleeves, two zippers over her large breasts and one at her crotch. She was still wearing the mask, but Nate recognized her now.

"What's going on here, Alice?" He tried to sound firm, but it was hard to feel anything but vulnerable as he lay pinned on his back below her. Taking off her mask, Alice looked at him coldly. Then she reached over and pinched his lips shut with her blue talons, silencing him.

"All secure!" she called back over her shoulder, and the redhead came prancing over to stand beside her. As Nate watched, she, too, removed her mask, and he was somehow not surprised to recognize Victoria. Victoria was also wearing a catsuit, black as midnight and cut low in the front to show off her deep cleavage. *Dive-inable*, thought Nate, beginning to feel slightly incoherent.

"Go ahead," ordered Victoria. "Examine him. Let's see what we've got here."

At first, Nate held his body rigid as Alice began to poke and prod. She'd gotten a stethoscope from somewhere and pressed the cold bell under his shirt, against his chest and belly. She shone a light in his eyes and ears, shoved a tongue depressor into his mouth—how foolish he felt saying "Ahh!"—and, casually reaching down his pants, she began a thorough investigation of his cock and balls. That was when Nate knew for sure that he wouldn't be going anywhere anytime soon. First of all, the straps were so tight that he was trapped, but more to the point, he couldn't deny that her ministrations, no matter how impersonal and rough, were speaking to him right where it counted. He might as well sit back and enjoy the ride.

"Ow!" Alice had pulled hard on his ball sac, disrupting the dreamy state he had entered when she had spent rather a long time playing with his foreskin, moving it up and down over his rapidly hardening shaft. Victoria laughed, and Alice pulled again, even harder, looking up at her friend for approval.

Victoria wrinkled her pert little nose. "He looks dirty to me," she said with disgust. "I think he needs to be cleaned out."

Alice giggled and moved to Victoria's side. Victoria pulled her close, running her hands up and down the latex encasing her body. They kissed, tongues mingling, Alice moaning. "Unzip for me, baby," murmured Victoria, seemingly forgetting about poor, dirty Nate. Alice reached up to liberate one magnificent nipple, hard and sweetly pink. Victoria parted her lips and engulfed her girlfriend's eager nub. Alice flung back her head, sighing, her blonde curls cascading down her back, beautiful against the red latex. Victoria was really getting into it, smearing lipstick over Alice's tit and making yummy noises as she sucked. Alice tossed her head from side to side, panting. Nate couldn't help it; he began to pant as well, his sore balls pulsing from the sight of the two catsuit-clad lovers.

Victoria raised her head and glared at him. "Sorry, baby," she said to Alice. "We need to take care of this filth right now."

Pouting a little, Alice nodded and left Nate's view, neglecting to zip up her suit. In fact, when she came back, she had unzipped the other side, and the sight of her nipples, rock hard and appetizing, distracted Nate so much that at first he couldn't focus on what she was holding. Then he saw it was an old-fashioned enema bag, the kind that used to fill him with fear as a kid when he saw it hung up in the shower in his grandparents' bathroom. It was an ugly, beige rubber pouch with a long hose ending in a nozzle. The nozzle looked uncommonly big.

"I'm sure you're as full of shit as any man," said Victoria conversationally, as she loosened his straps, positioned him on his side, then quickly did up the restraints before he could get any bright ideas about making a dash for it. She took the enema bag from Alice, hefted it expertly, then moved around behind Nate. Giving him no time at all to try and breathe or get used to the idea, she parted his asscheeks with an unforgiving hand and shoved in the super-sized nozzle. He yelped and tried to slide away, but he was well secured and there was nothing to do but take it. Squeezing his eyes shut, he groaned as a whole bag of freezing water rushed into his protesting ass.

Victoria yanked out the nozzle and slapped his buttcheeks,

hard. Nate gasped, certain he was going to spill, and even more certain that things would not go well for him if he did. Sure enough, Victoria slapped and scratched and pulled at him even harder. "You hold that," she commanded. Her strong hands suddenly grabbed for his dick, massaging it back to hardness. "I know you can do it," she said with authority. "I know you'll do it for me."

"Yes," groaned Nate, overwhelmed with sensation. Opening his eyes to gaze on her stern features, he knew he would do everything in his power to obey her. He clenched his asscheeks together as tightly as he could, closed his eyes again and held it. And held it. When he was at the limit of his capabilities, he opened his eyes and looked around, desperately. He expected to see his tormentors watching him, enjoying his agony, but they were nowhere in sight.

"Please!" he whispered, and Victoria came stalking over, frowning.

"You'd better not mess the table, boy," she said, then relented somewhat, undid the straps and allowed him to stagger to his feet. For an awful moment, Nate thought he was going to let go right there in the middle of the floor. The look in Victoria's eyes told him she wouldn't mind at all if he did, as it would give her more reason to torture him in some other, fiendish manner. At the last moment, though, he spied the bathroom and managed to stagger in that direction, hampered by his pants, which were down around his ankles. There was no door to close, and at first he didn't care, just grateful that he'd made it to the toilet. But when he looked up and saw both women right there, hands on hips, watching him avidly, he trembled with shame.

"Again," said Victoria, when he had voided himself completely. They filled him up with that frigid water once more, right there as he lay on the nasty gritty tiles of the bathroom.

With no more thought of escape, Nate steeled himself to endure whatever came his way. At last, Victoria declared him to be "as clean as he'll ever get." They stripped him naked, and allowed him to return to his table, where they let him lie unstrapped as they kissed and fondled each other's titties. Nate didn't think he would be allowed to touch his dick, but they looked so incredible as they rubbed up against each other, Alice's pink nipples poking out to meet Victoria's spit-covered tongue, that he couldn't resist trying. Sure enough, Victoria noticed.

"Man-toy is not to touch his horny little cock!" she snapped, and then, in a nicer voice, "It's time for his ass-reaming, wouldn't you say, Alice, sweetie?"

Alice jumped up and down, squealing and clapping her hands. She seemed to take extreme pleasure in the devious acts her girlfriend continued to dream up. She ran into the bathroom and Nate could hear water running—oh please, not another enema! —but then he was distracted by Victoria, who had retrieved a harness and a huge, shiny pink dildo from a drawer in his table. She buckled the harness on over her catsuit, coming close to him, thrusting the dildo in his face and slapping his cheeks with it, all the time laughing her low throaty laugh.

"You go ahead, baby," Victoria said to Alice, who immediately started doing something at the end of the table, near Nate's feet. He couldn't pay attention to it, because Victoria continued to torment him with her tool, which was fatter than any real dick he'd ever seen, including his own not-too-shabby piece of equipment. In her usual perfunctory manner, she rammed the disgusting thing past his lips and down his throat. Nate did his best to take it, although its painful girth made him gag. He remembered Victoria had talked about fucking his ass, and whimpered at the thought of this monster invading him. His pitiful sounds only caused Victoria to thrust more vigorously, and he thought he could hear Alice snickering.

Nate was vaguely aware that something cold was being slapped onto one of his ankles, but he couldn't concentrate with Victoria fucking his mouth and muttering angrily about how he was a piss-poor cocksucker. She finally pulled out and joined Alice.

Nate managed to raise his battered head to look down at them. They were in the process of encasing him in a plaster cast. He didn't have time to ponder the ramifications of this fully, as just then Alice appeared beside him. Smiling almost kindly, she bent over and dangled a luscious tit just above his lips. By the time he had sucked himself silly, his legs were completely immobilized in plaster, and Victoria had gleefully started on his arms and chest.

Nate felt like a mummy; he had to fight the claustrophobia brought on by not being able to move at all. The girls had left his ass, dick and balls uncovered, with just enough play at his waist so they could turn him from side to side, onto his back or onto his belly. The rest of him, up to his neck, was covered with a thick, chalky, slightly sweet-smelling plaster cast.

Once the plaster was completely dry, Nate got his ass-fucking. Alice held his legs over his head, exposing his tender asshole and allowing Victoria to tear into him with that diabolically fat dildo, the only mercy being that she first allowed Alice to slick it up with some lube. Still, Nate couldn't help sobbing just a little as she pried him open. Soon, though, she had worked up a good rhythm and Nate was moaning with pleasure. He could feel his balls tightening, on the verge of a really good come. As if she could read his mind, Victoria pulled out with a nasty sucking sound and shoved him off the table. He crashed to the hard floor, unable to stop the fall.

Now Alice stood over him, her stiletto boots dangerously

close to his ears. She unzipped and spread wide, squatting over his face, supported by Victoria, who sat behind her.

"Eat her good," said Victoria, and Nate eagerly lifted his face into the swamp of her pussy. The latex had done its work and the smell of pussy juice, pussy sweat, piss and the fug from her sweaty crack behind was heady and delicious. Nate took a deep breath, relishing it, then plunged in eagerly, lapping at her slick slit with everything he had. If he satisfied her girlfriend now, he could only hope and pray that Victoria—the evil goddess—might allow him to worship at her red-hot cunt later. In the meantime, he ate out Alice as if his life depended on it—for all he knew, in his befuddled state, it did!

Ignoring the zipper, which cut into his cheeks, he ran long, loving strokes up and down her lightly furred pussy lips, playfully twirling his tongue at her opening, then moving back to slurp at her clit. Judging from her moans, he was pleasing her, but he didn't dare stop. Faster and faster he moved his tongue as she smeared her juicy pussy on his face, bucking against him. He had his tongue deep inside her when she came.

And then the women got up, switched off the lights and left him. He was alone for what seemed like ages. It could have been a few hours, or a week. He drifted in and out of sleep, constantly on edge, constantly aroused. He thought he was dreaming when the smell of pussy entered his nose, but no, it was Victoria, mercifully draping her plump, shaved box over his face, allowing him to service her in the best way he knew how. She came, practically suffocating him as she ground her greedy cunt into his mouth and nose. Then she kicked him over onto his stomach and allowed him to hump the floor until he came, yelling and swearing. And then he was alone again.

Nate jerked awake when the lights were flipped on. "Oh, dear!" he heard someone say, in a soft, alarmed voice. Patty stepped into view, so reassuring in her formfitting yoga outfit, the look on her face so kind and worried that Nate felt a rush of hope. "What have those girls been up to?" she murmured, bending down to get a closer look. Nate was intensely embarrassed for his yoga teacher to see him like this, but then he realized she had been driving the car and must be in on the whole thing. Still, when she asked him if she could help, he jumped at the chance and asked if she could get him out of the cast.

"Oh, poor Nate, of course!" She got a little saw, the light gleaming on its blade, and turned it on. The buzz filled Nate with dread.

"I don't really know how to use this, but I'll give it a try!" The buzzing got louder as she brought the saw close to the cast on his chest. He felt the vibration as the blade bit into the plaster.

"No!" he shouted, but Patty just kept on hacking away. She had managed to get off about half of the cast, nicking him severely in the process, when Victoria and Alice came strolling back into the room, arms around each other.

Patty dropped the saw, still buzzing, and the three women embraced, stroking each other, kissing and cooing.

"Well, how do you like what we've done with him?" asked Victoria, finally, waving a proprietary arm at Nate.

"Not a bad package," said Patty. "I had a lot of fun starting to unwrap him." All three of them giggled.

"Oh, I don't think we're quite finished with him yet," said Victoria, licking her lips and fastening her ruthless gaze on Nate. "He does a fair job eating pussy, and his hungry little asshole makes for a passably good fuck. Speaking of which, did you bring the little present I got you?"

"Of course!" Patty dropped her pants to reveal that she was packing a purple dildo the size of a Minuteman missile. The next thing Nate knew, Alice had popped open the lube, and Patty was positioning him so that she could get at his ass. In spite of himself, he could feel himself opening for her, allowing her in.

"When she's done, we have a few more tasks for you, Natey baby," he heard Alice say loftily. Like the good boy he was, Nate nodded his head eagerly and moved his ass on Patty's monstrous dildo. He had to admit, just before he began to lose his head entirely, that, way more than anything he could have pulled out of his bag of tricks, this had turned out to be a fucking amazing roller coaster of a first date.

OF HUMAN BONDAGE

Rachel Kramer Bussel

When Maya settles herself over Dylan's face, planting her pussy right on top of his waiting lips, she's not just giving herself over to a glorious cunnilingus session, she's also keeping him in place for me, making sure he doesn't move—just as I've instructed her. The three of us live together and love each other—and make love to each other. Well, *fuck* each other would be more accurate, and, to be even more accurate—I fuck *both* of them. Oh, that doesn't mean Dylan's cock and Maya's hands haven't been inside me countless times, but I'm the mastermind, the girl in charge, giving them cues, watching them writhe, utterly in control even when my body is losing control.

We have an extremely well-stocked toy closet (yes, enough to fill an actual closet), but even though I have all manner of objects I could use to pin Dylan down, my favorite bondage equipment comes in the form of the six-foot frame of my favorite tall, busty redhead. It's funny to me that Maya is pure sub through and through—I can see her shiver when I so much as look at her the right way—because she's so statuesque, a beautiful quivering Amazon. Dylan's no slouch, either, at two inches taller than her. I'm the short one, at only five six, but what I lack in height I make up for in other ways.

"Wrap your thighs more tightly around his face," I instruct Maya, smiling as she does my bidding. It's a win-win for me: she holds him in place, and I get to watch her pretend like she's in control, until his powerful tongue works its magic and she comes all over him. When we first brought her into the fold, she had trouble believing he really liked to be smothered by her wetness. She did it when I told her to, but now she takes her own kind of delight in pleasing him and me at the same time, fully aware of the magic she holds between her legs.

Today I have a challenge for him. Dylan is going to hold himself in place, a fitting "punishment" for a man who tends to be impatient at all times, even in bed, which is precisely why he likes to have his face muffled by her muff—or at least, one of the reasons. "Get up for a second," I tell her. Perfect sub that she is, she doesn't hesitate. "Dylan, hold yourself by the ankles." I know he's flexible enough to do this with ease, and in moments, I'm staring at the pucker of his ass, spread open before me. He won't be able to hold this for too long, but that's okay; I can be quick when I want to. Besides, seeing him trembling right from the start, holding on for dear life, clinging to not just his own limbs but his servitude, is a wondrous gift.

"Go back to giving him a pussy bath, Maya." Neither of them have to be silent—I'm not that kind of domme—but they are so focused on my words they don't need to speak. The tremor that races through Dylan as he multitasks, keeping his grip on his ankles and making his tongue useful as she rides his face, is one I want to feel up close, skin on skin.

I quickly don the special panties I wear when I fuck him, the ones that have a hole just for the cock that only ever goes in his ass (I have others I use on all of Maya's holes). When I put it on, he knows what's going to happen; he also knows I'm just mean enough not to give it to him when he asks, so he doesn't bother, but I've learned to see the signs, the desire bubbling up from within. I like to give him what he wants, with a twist.

I can't see his face, blocked as it is by Maya's pink lips and tufts of orange hair, as I slide the cock in place, nor when I lube it up. I have to imagine his tongue diving inside Maya, except when she raises herself up, only to rub her pussy all over his face. I lean forward to give her a deep kiss before putting a hand on each of Dylan's cheeks. I don't need to get him any more open than he already is, but I like the way Dylan shudders when I hold him wide open. His ass is pulsing, clenching at air, beckoning me inside. I push the head in and see his hands slip just enough to make me pause.

"You want me to fuck you, don't you? If you do, then you'll keep your hands where they belong. I'm giving you the chance to hold yourself, rather than being strung up like someone who can't be trusted. You don't want to break that trust now, do you, Dylan?" I say it in a singsong, sweet but stern tone, one that commands and corrects, sweeping away any potential objections. The truth is, Dylan and Maya both trust me to lead them, just as I trust them to follow. It's a symbiotic relationship.

Symbiotic is also a perfect description of what happens when my slick cock slides all the way inside him. I lean forward and kiss Maya again, bringing my hands up to join Dylan's, pushing his legs closer toward his shoulders. "I want a taste too," I murmur, and Maya rises, maneuvering so I can lick her in full view of Dylan. He moans, the kind of moan you'd think would mean he wants to join in, if you didn't know how much he likes being denied.

I bite Maya's lower lip and ease back, watching the dick slide in and out of Dylan. Without my prodding, Maya presses her knees lightly against his neck, sinking down onto him. This time, he clutches himself more tightly, digging in the way I've seen him grab the headboard or bite into a pillow, relishing being "made" to stay in place.

"Now put your tits in his mouth," I say as I plunge deep inside. Dylan's grip loosens a little, but one warning cluck of my tongue and he's holding himself tight once again. Maya slithers around so she's leaning forward over him, pushing her breasts together to fit both nipples between his lips. His poor cock is hard and starting to leak, so I take pity on him and wrap my hand around it while his mouth tugs at each of Maya's nubs in turn.

The feel of him in my hand is too distracting to keep fucking him. I pull out and slip off the panties. "Maya, come help me." Then I'm the one pinning Dylan down with my weight. While he licks my pussy, she and I jointly get his cock nice and wet, her tongue at the base, with the tip between my lips. When his hands reach for my hips, I let him. There are some things you can't do when you're tied up. He tugs me close and buries himself in me while I sink down until my lips meet Maya's. Dylan's been trained to wait for me, and his tongue has been trained to know exactly what I like. Soon I'm coming, which gives him permission to do the same. I pull away just as he erupts, watching with a smile.

I move so I'm lying next to Dylan, then grab Maya by her hair and lead her tongue to all the places that need to be cleaned. "Good girl. You're next," I tell her, already picturing Dylan holding her arms behind her back while I use a vibrator on her. Or maybe I'll have him straddle her and fuck her tits while I drive her wild with the new plug-in model I just got. There are so many possibilities, which is why my human toys will always be my favorites.

ABOUT THE AUTHORS

LN BEY has lived in various suburbs and city centers across the Midwest and West, playing kinky married games, writing kinky stories and serving demanding cats.

EMILY BINGHAM (queanofrope.com) is a storyteller, rope bondage instructor and consent activist. The only thing she loves more than words is rope. Her stories have appeared in a number of anthologies including *Serving Him: Sexy Stories of Submission* and *Best Bondage Erotica 2011* and *2014*.

ROBERT BLACK is a writer and editor with a background in newspapers, advertising, corporate communications and textbooks. He is a lifetime resident of Rhode Island. His daughter Lia is also a writer; her twin brother Chris is a musician. This is Robert's first published work of fiction.

SHENOA CARROLL-BRADD lives in Southern California with her brother and dancing dog, on a street where she can see both mountains and palm trees. She writes whatever catches her fancy, from erotica, to horror and fantasy. Say hello on Twitter @ShenoaSays.

ELIZABETH COLDWELL (elizabethcoldwell.wordpress.com) lives and writes in London. Her stories have appeared in numerous anthologies, including *Best Bondage Erotica 2011, 2012, 2013* and *2014*.

CORVIDAE is a proud scientist and avid kinkster. Her work has been featured in *The Big Book of Submission: 69 Kinky Tales* and she is a regular contributor to the Erotica Readers and Writers Association. She generally lives in California and occasionally blogs at corvidaedream.wordpress.com.

JENNE DAVIS, head honcho at clitical.com, sees herself as more of a gatekeeper than a webmistress. While she does own several whips, she would rather spend her time writing about them than wielding them. Jenne believes that sex is about sharing and open communication.

LUCY FELTHOUSE (lucyfelthouse.co.uk) is a very busy woman! She writes erotica and erotic romance in a variety of subgenres, lengths and pairings, and has over one hundred publications to her name, with many more in the pipeline. These include several *Best* anthologies from Cleis Press.

NICHELLE GREGORY (simplysexystories.com) has penned fifteen erotically charged books for Totally Bound, including *Ashes to Flames, Talk Sexy* and *Soul Sweet*. She enjoys bringing believable, diverse characters to life that thrill and excite her readers with gorgeous alpha heroes and divine heroines in magical, exotic, sexy scenarios.

JODIE GRIFFIN (jodiegriffin.com) loves chocolate and alliterative titles, sees the dirty side in pretty much everything and needs more hours in every day. She writes naughty tales about nice girls and the men who love them.

ELISE HEPNER (elisehepner.com) writes smutty goodness for Ellora's Cave, Xcite and Secret Cravings Publishing. She's appeared in several Cleis anthologies including *Gotta Have It: 69 Stories of Sudden Sex* and *Best Bondage Erotica 2012*. She lives with her husband and two clingy kitties in Maryland.

ANNABEL JOSEPH (annabeljoseph.com) is a multi-published kinky novelist whose stories celebrate the complexity and romance of erotic power exchange. When she's not penning hot BDSM tales, she's on Twitter discussing orgasm denial, trapeze sex and other such vital topics.

D. L. KING (dlkingerotica.blogspot.com) is the editor of anthologies such as *Carnal Machines* (IPPY gold medal winner), *Under Her Thumb* and *The Harder She Comes* (Lambda Literary Award winner and also IPPY gold medalist). Her stories can be found in *Bound for Trouble, Fast Girls* and *Luscious*, among many others.

ANNABETH LEONG (annabethleong.blogspot.com) writes erotica of many flavors. Her work has appeared in more than thirty anthologies, including *Best Bondage Erotica 2013* and *2014* (Cleis Press). Her stand-alone titles include *One Flesh* (Storm Moon Press), *The Fugitive's Sexy Brother* (Ellora's Cave) and *Untouched* (Sweetmeats Press).

SOMMER MARSDEN (sommermarsden.blogspot.com) is a professional dirty word writer, gluten free baker, sock addict, fat-wiener-dog walker, expert procrastinator. Called "one of the top storytellers in the erotic genre" by Violet Blue, Sommer's the author of numerous erotic novels including *Restricted Release, Boys Next Door, Restless Spirit* and *Lost in You.*

ROB ROSEN (therobrosen.net), author of the novels *Sparkle: The Queerest Book You'll Ever Love, Divas Las Vegas, Hot Lava, Southern Fried, Queerwolf* and *Vamp*, and editor of the anthologies *Lust in Time* and *Men of the Manor*, has had short stories featured in more than 180 anthologies.

TIM RUDOLPH is the owner of a dirty mind and a number two pencil, which have combined to produce stories for Oysters and Chocolate, *The Mammoth Book of Quick and Dirty Erotica* and *The Mammoth Book of Urban Erotic Confessions*. He lives and writes in Santa Cruz.

ERIN SPILLANE always has at least one crazy idea running through her head and she realized it would be easier and safer to write them down. Sometimes, anyway. She's a dreamer. Follow her on Twitter @Erin_Spillane.

L. C. SPOERING (lcspoering.com) lives and writes in Denver, Colorado. Her work has appeared in anthologies with Cleis Press, Lady Lit and Seal Press, as well as *The Dying Goose* literary magazine, and her first book, *After Life Lessons*, coauthored with Laila Blake, was released in 2014.

ANNA WATSON hates yoga and spent over a year in a half body cast when she was but a wee chick. For more stories, see

Best Lesbian Erotica 2015, *No Safewords*, *Slaphappy/Mrs. M* and *Me and My Boi*. With a colleague, she recently launched Laz-E-Femme Press. Kick off your pumps and read!

DADDY X always wanted to be a dirty old man. Despite Catholic school, a steel mill, Haight Ashbury, drugs, alcoholism, stroke, cancer, liver transplant, chemo, robbery at gunpoint, and a triple bypass, he's grown old. Now he's gonna get dirty. Daddy lives with Momma X, a lop-eared hound and two cats.

ABOUT THE EDITOR

RACHEL KRAMER BUSSEL (rachelkramerbussel.com) is a New Jersey-based author, editor and blogger. She's the author of the essay collection *Sex & Cupcakes*, and has edited over fifty books of erotica, including *The Big Book of Orgasms; The Big Book of Submission; Hungry for More; Anything for You: Erotica for Kinky Couples; Baby Got Back: Anal Erotica; Suite Encounters; Going Down; Irresistible; Gotta Have It; Obsessed; Women in Lust; Surrender; Orgasmic; Cheeky Spanking Stories; Bottoms Up; Spanked: Red-Cheeked Erotica; Fast Girls; Do Not Disturb; Going Down; Tasting Him; Tasting Her; Please, Sir; Please, Ma'am; He's on Top; She's on Top; Caught Looking; Hide and Seek* and is *Best Bondage Erotica* series editor. Her anthologies have won eight IPPY (Independent Publisher) Awards, and *Surrender* won the National Leather Association Samois Anthology Award. Her work has been published in over one hundred anthologies, including *Best American Erotica 2004* and *2006*. She wrote the popular "Lusty Lady" column for the *Village Voice* and currently writes the "Let's Get It On" column for *Philadelphia City Paper*. Rachel has written for *AVN, Bust,* cleansheets.com, *Cosmopolitan, Curve,* The Daily Beast, elle.com, thefrisky.com, *Glamour*, *Harper's Bazaar,* Huffington Post, *Inked*, Mediabistro, *Newsday, New York Post, New York Observer, Penthouse,* The Root, Salon, *San Francisco Chronicle,* time.com, *Time Out New York* and *Zink,* among others. She has appeared on *The Gayle King Show*, *The Martha Stewart Show*, *The Berman and Berman Show*, NY1 and Showtime's *Family Business*. She hosted the popular In the Flesh Erotic Reading Series, featuring readers from Susie Bright to Zane, and speaks at conferences, does readings and teaches erotic writing workshops across the country. She blogs at lustylady.blogspot.com.

Many More than Fifty Shades of Erotica

Please, Sir
Erotic Stories of Female Submission
Edited by Rachel Kramer Bussel

If you liked *Fifty Shades of Grey,* you'll love the explosive stories of *Please, Sir.* These damsels delight in the pleasures of taking risks to be rewarded by the men who know their deepest desires. Find out why nothing is as hot as the power of the words "Please, Sir."
ISBN 978-1-57344-389-0 $14.95

Yes, Sir
Erotic Stories of Female Submission
Edited by Rachel Kramer Bussel

Bound, gagged or spanked—or controlled with just a glance—these lucky women experience the breathtaking thrills of sexual submission. *Yes, Sir* shows that pleasure is best when dispensed by a firm hand.
ISBN 978-1-57344-310-4 $15.95

He's on Top
Erotic Stories of Male Dominance and Female Submission
Edited by Rachel Kramer Bussel

As true tops, the bossy hunks in these stories understand that BDSM is about exulting in power that is freely yielded. These kinky stories celebrate women who know exactly what they want.
ISBN 978-1-57344-270-1 $14.95

Best Bondage Erotica 2014
Edited by Rachel Kramer Bussel

Let *Best Bondage Erotica 2014* be your kinky playbook to erotic restraint—from silk ties and rope to shiny cuffs, blindfolds and so much more. These stories of forbidden desire will captivate, shock and arouse you.
978-1-62778-012-4 $15.95

Luscious
Stories of Anal Eroticism
Edited by Alison Tyler

Discover all the erotic possibilities that exist between the sheets and between the cheeks in this daring collection. "Alison Tyler is an author to rely on for steamy, sexy page turners! Try her!"—Powell's Books
ISBN 978-1-57344-760-7 $15.95

*** Free book of equal or lesser value. Shipping and applicable sales tax extra.**
Cleis Press • (800) 780-2279 • orders@cleispress.com
www.cleispress.com

Red Hot Erotic Romance

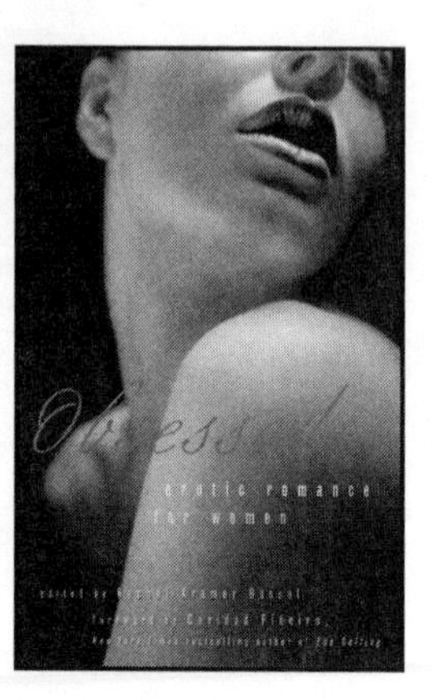

Obsessed
Erotic Romance for Women
Edited by Rachel Kramer Bussel

These stories sizzle with the kind of obsession that is fueled by our deepest desires, the ones that hold couples together, the ones that haunt us and don't let go. Whether just-blooming passions, rekindled sparks or reinvented relationships, these lovers put the object of their obsession first.
ISBN 978-1-57344-718-8 $14.95

Passion
Erotic Romance for Women
Edited by Rachel Kramer Bussel

Love and sex have always been intimately intertwined—and *Passion* shows just how delicious the possibilities are when they mingle in this sensual collection edited by award-winning author Rachel Kramer Bussel.
ISBN 978-1-57344-415-6 $14.95

Girls Who Bite
Lesbian Vampire Erotica
Edited by Delilah Devlin

Bestselling romance writer Delilah Devlin and her contributors add fresh girl-on-girl blood to the pantheon of the paranormal. The stories in *Girls Who Bite* are varied, unexpected, and soul-scorching.
ISBN 978-1-57344-715-7 $14.95

Irresistible
Erotic Romance for Couples
Edited by Rachel Kramer Bussel

This prolific editor has gathered the most popular fantasies and created a sizzling, no-holds-barred collection of explicit encounters in which couples turn their deepest desires into reality.
978-1-57344-762-1 $14.95

Heat Wave
Hot, Hot, Hot Erotica
Edited by Alison Tyler

What could be sexier or more seductive than bare, sun-warmed skin? Bestselling erotica author Alison Tyler gathers explicit stories of summer sex bursting with the sweet eroticism of swimsuits, sprinklers, and ripe strawberries.
ISBN 978-1-57344-710-2 $15.95

*** Free book of equal or lesser value. Shipping and applicable sales tax extra.**
Cleis Press • (800) 780-2279 • orders@cleispress.com
www.cleispress.com

Bestselling Erotica for Couples

Sweet Life
Erotic Fantasies for Couples
Edited by Violet Blue

Your ticket to a front row seat for first-time spankings, breathtaking role-playing scenes, sex parties, women who strap it on and men who love to take it, not to mention threesomes of every combination.
ISBN 978-1-57344-133-9 $14.95

Sweet Life 2
Erotic Fantasies for Couples
Edited by Violet Blue

"This is a we-did-it-you-can-too anthology of real couples playing out their fantasies."
—Lou Paget, author of *365 Days of Sensational Sex*
ISBN 978-1-57344-167-4 $15.95

Sweet Love
Erotic Fantasies for Couples
Edited by Violet Blue

"If you ever get a chance to try out your number-one fantasies in real life—and I assure you, there will be more than one—say yes. It's well worth it. May this book, its adventurous authors, and the daring and satisfied characters be your guiding inspiration."—Violet Blue
ISBN 978-1-57344-381-4 $14.95

Afternoon Delight
Erotica for Couples
Edited by Alison Tyler

"Alison Tyler evokes a world of heady sensuality where fantasies are fearlessly explored and dreams gloriously realized."
—Barbara Pizio, Executive Editor, *Penthouse Variations*
ISBN 978-1-57344-341-8 $14.95

Three-Way
Erotic Stories
Edited by Alison Tyler

"Three means more of everything. Maybe I'm greedy, but when it comes to sex, I like more. More fingers. More tongues. More limbs. More tangling and wrestling on the mattress."
ISBN 978-1-57344-193-3 $15.95

*** Free book of equal or lesser value. Shipping and applicable sales tax extra.**
Cleis Press • (800) 780-2279 • orders@cleispress.com
www.cleispress.com

Ordering is easy! Call us toll free or fax us to place your MC/VISA order.
You can also mail the order form below with payment to:
Cleis Press, 2246 Sixth St., Berkeley, CA 94710.

ORDER FORM

QTY	TITLE	PRICE
	SUBTOTAL	
	SHIPPING	
	SALES TAX	
	TOTAL	

Add $3.95 postage/handling for the first book ordered and $1.00 for each additional book. Outside North America, please contact us for shipping rates. California residents add 9% sales tax. Payment in U.S. dollars only.

★ Free book of equal or lesser value. Shipping and applicable sales tax extra.

Cleis Press • Phone: (800) 780-2279 • Fax: (510) 845-8001
orders@cleispress.com • www.cleispress.com
You'll find more great books on our website

Follow us on Twitter @cleispress • Friend/fan us on Facebook